DON'T STOP
BELIEVING

MIDLIFE MULLIGAN, BOOK THREE

BY EVE LANGLAIS

PROLOGUE

THE BEAST WAS DEAD. NOT REALLY A SURPRISE given the aquatic monster had outlived its purpose. The creature, named Maddy by the humans, had fought long and hard against their dominion. It took years after its capture before it did their bidding and helped them retrieve the muddy remains of the source. Hard to believe the sludge that Maddy guarded inside her underwater cave was part of the key to unlocking the magic they'd lost.

They dredged everything they could from the lake, down to the smallest speck. Packaged hundreds of bottles bearing the inert source.

Not long now. The bottles had been distributed to the new residents expanding the town of Cambden and its surrounding areas. A grubby hamlet that didn't come close to resembling the grand cities of old that they'd once ruled. They'd gone from royalty to paupers, but their time was about to come again.

Leviathan regarded the body at his feet. Dead because it failed him. Jude—a human suit he'd worn from time to time—had outlived his use.

A good thing he always had a few spare vessels to jump into. He kicked the body into the water lapping at the interior pier. He didn't worry about it being found given the rapacious fish he'd seeded in the water. Always hungry for fresh meat.

As Leviathan strode from the loading dock, now silent with the machines turned off, he noticed with satisfaction that they'd finished ahead of schedule. Now he only had to play his repulsive part, and then he'd be the one to lead them into the new world.

The one to wield the most magic.

As he entered the reception area, his gaze tracked directly to those passing through. His stride quickened, though not as long as he liked. The vessel he'd taken over was not to his usual standards; however, it suited his purpose for the moment. Especially once he made some subtle modifications.

Leviathan smirked at the other princes, only

eleven left of the original seventeen who fled death in their world. With little time to scout, and the planets ill aligned, they'd had to settle for Earth, a place with suitable hosts for their consciousness, if lacking in magic.

"Are you working together to wrest control from me?" He was only half mocking. He'd not made it to this point by underestimating his competition.

"If you want to drive, then go ahead. The end result will be the same. Magic for all," Soneillon pointed out.

Leviathan snorted. "You would be blasé, given my sources say you've been working on the witch's daughter."

The prince shrugged. "You failed. Time for someone else to have a turn."

"I had her," he argued. As Jude, he had fucked the daughter then thought he could make the act with the mother more palatable by inviting her to join them.

"And then lost her," Astaroth said with a laugh. "What is the delay? Does the body you chose to use have issues?"

"My cock works just fine. It's her. The witch." He grimaced.

"If it's so repugnant then, move aside for someone else," Astaroth suggested.

"Like you? Is there anything you won't fornicate with?" Leviathan growled, growing tired of the deal he'd made with the other remaining royals. This uneasy alliance was only born out of necessity. Centuries of seeking the source and seeing themselves dwindle in number. And then finally the clue that changed everything.

A lake hiding a lost treasure guarded by a formidable witch.

But they had time to get past her defenses and tame the beast guarding it. The alignment they'd been waiting for was moments away. Soon, they would take back their power.

And then Leviathan would kill everyone, so he didn't have to share it.

1

Not long after Christmas, I had the lake monster dream. A thing I used to dread. Now, it saddened me. Maddy, the creature people claimed lived in Cambden's lake, was gone.

The pebbled beach marching into the water held no ominous shade or shape. No unusual humps or ripples marred the surface of the lake. No more nuclear glowing either.

The monster had passed away, and I missed it. I woke sniffling. Sad.

What is wrong with me? Why would anyone miss the terror that Maddy used to bring? I mean the darned thing used to eat me practically each time I closed my eyes.

Except in my last dream of Maddy, when the beast looked sick and dying. Had my subconscious killed my imaginary beast? Perhaps it was a symbolic thing that had to do with my burgeoning sense of self-empowerment. I'd transformed from a housewife and a doormat. Gotten out of a toxic relationship with a man who despised me.

And I mean despise.

Martin had set my house on fire. With me in it. That kind of left a bitter taste in my mouth, which often flipped into the sour flavor of guilt because I'd yet to give a damn he'd died.

Martin had turned into a mean old man, and I was glad he was gone. Life was better than I could remember. I greeted the day now instead of dreading it.

With that thought, I sprang out of bed, delighted to find the sheets dry. No menopausal sweats in the middle of the night where I was stripping the bed and taking a cold shower. Twice in the last week it happened. Nothing during the day yet. I assumed it was coming and wondered if they had a *Jaws*-like theme song for the menopause symptoms that liked to pounce at inconvenient times. Although I was digging the silver in my hair. I thought of it as natural highlights.

Joints popped as I stretched, and I jiggled a bit more than a person should as I made my bed. A new thing I'd started doing. I'd spent most of my adult life, say from when I moved out of my grand-ma's house until recently, leaving it a mess. Then I discovered the joys of climbing into a neatly made bed. Every morning I now yanked up the sheets and comforter, fluffed my pillow on top, tucked my jammies under it, then walked in my underwear into the bathroom.

Naked and super self-conscious despite being alone. However, a book I'd been reading said feeling more confident meant accepting myself as I was. The whole love-yourself thing, which took effort.

What helped give me a boost was knowing I had a busy day ahead at my store. People on their holiday breaks between Christmas and New Year would be out spending, looking for Boxing Day— now weeklong—deals. I'd printed out some new signs to put in my store overnight.

In the bathroom, I stepped on the scale and blinked at the digital display of a number I'd not seen since my first pregnancy.

My lower lip wobbled. With happiness. It felt good to reach a goal I'd set for myself. Yay for me!

I showered, and blow-dried my silver-streaked hair as I readied for work. Some people might hate their jobs, but I loved mine. There was something exciting about going out in the world and doing something. Supporting myself. Providing to society.

Hell, I had to pay taxes! Which some might complain about but to me was a sign of how far I'd come. I didn't depend on anyone.

I was in charge of me.

Booyah.

Spirits high, I skipped down the stairs, now wider than before. The house had changed to suit me. Although why I'd need a wide set of stairs when it was just me using them was baffling.

Wait. Was my house trying to tell me something?

Things with my kind-of-boyfriend Darryl were heating up. He'd kissed me again when he came by last night with his dog, Herbie, and a fistful of flowers offered with a grin. I might have smiled just as stupidly back before I got slobbered on by the biggest puppy you ever saw.

I laughed like a fiend as Darryl swore, "For fuck's sake, you mangy mutt. Get off her."

The commotion brought Winnie, my daughter, who declared the dog her new best friend and then kidnapped him for a walk.

I wondered if Darryl had planned for that to happen since it would give us alone time. After all, his excuse to visit me was pretty flimsy. He claimed it was to show me some stuff he'd found to put up for sale in my shop. He could have just dropped the goods off when I was at work, but instead he came knocking on my door.

He didn't stay long and apologized profusely while collecting his dog from Winnie, who'd had the misfortune of bumping into our grumpy neighbor, Jace. Darryl promised he'd see me soon.

I couldn't wait. I'd been smiling so much lately my cheeks hurt. This was happiness.

My life was a box of chocolates with each flavor a day that became my new favorite one. My enjoyment was marred only by a foreboding that something wicked was coming to run me over.

Dun. Dun. Dun.

Could anyone else hear the ominous music playing? Why couldn't I enjoy the moment? Seize the day? Why did I have to constantly think negatively? Did I want the drama?

As I hit the main floor of my cottage—that was sliding into a mid-sized house—it was to see my son at the sink, rinsing his dishes—not something he'd ever done when he lived at home. But it appeared moving out on his own gave him a better appreciation of the kind of help I'd hoped for when we all lived together.

At times, I felt bad at how often I got mad at my kids. Getting caught up in stupid shit that had no importance, like wanting them to clean their rooms, stack the dirty stuff inside the dishwasher, put their laundry away. And my biggest peeve, shoes and socks all over the front hall.

Now some would say that yelling paid off because look at my kids now. They might be living with me at the moment, but they were model roommates. However, new me, wiser me, wished I'd shown more patience. I loved my kids but didn't always express it in the best ways. My personal misery led to me sharing it. In hindsight, I could see the despair in my actions. For a while, I'd forgotten how to look for the joy.

But I was learning. Every day I got a little better at it. The biggest thing I'd learned? Start your day with a bright disposition.

"Morning, fruit of my loins," I chirped as I sailed into the kitchen.

My son cast me a glance behind a thick hank of hair. He'd let it grow out, along with a beard. My baby boy sported a scruffy jaw. "You're in a good mood."

"It's a beautiful morning." Spoken by someone who'd yet to set foot outside.

Geoff glanced at the window. "It's overcast, and the forecast is saying to expect a few inches of snow."

"Then it's a good day for you to game with your

friends," I announced. When he was a teen, I worried about him playing them too much and yet set no limit on television watching. I saw no harm in the fake drama on screen. Back then, video games were the rock and roll of that generation, ruining kids.

And then I discovered the joy of apps on my phone. Why had I ever limited him? I now understood the calming nature of an electronic game. I'd been Candy Crush-ing enough I was level 705.

"Gaming requires a computer or, at the very least, a television not built in the 1980s and a video game console, Mom," he said with amusement.

I glanced around at my house and sent it a thought. *You heard that. I don't suppose you can conjure those up?*

The house didn't exactly reply. It never spoke per se, but it did provide. Be jealous. I had a magical home that just wanted to please, and it dusted!

"I might just be able to wrangle something for you," I said aloud. If the house couldn't do it, then maybe I could buy something in town.

His brows rose. "Don't tell me you've got an Atari kicking around?"

"You better hope not, because I will challenge

you to a game of Pong and kick your butt." I did a little victory move that had him snorting.

"You are so weird."

It melted my heart to hear him say that because when he was young, he used to say that when I'd do silly things to make him smile.

"Not as weird as you," I chanted in reply with a wink.

"You off to the shop today?"

I nodded. He'd tried to help out the first day, but selling antiques just didn't have the same appeal to him as it did for me. He'd nodded off to sleep and had almost fallen off the stool behind the counter.

"What time you finishing? I'll make dinner."

I wasn't about to say no. "Five-ish?" I said. With it being winter and dark early, the store traffic dried up quick late afternoon. Which reminded me. "I'll have to take a rain check. I told Trish I'd meet her at the diner."

"Then it's time to test your local pizza delivery." He rubbed his hands together.

I laughed. "That is way too much excitement for cheese on a flat bread."

"I've seen you with steak. Don't talk."

"Don't talk smack about a nice bacon-wrapped six-ounce tenderloin." I just about drooled.

"Give me a fatty rib eye and a baked potato."

"Mmm. Rib eye." I wasn't picky about my meat. Bring the meat. I'd eat all the meat.

I might have said that out loud, because my son cleared his throat. "Are you hungry or something?"

"Nope. A coffee is all I need." I prepped my travel mug and saluted him as I headed for the door. My stockinged feet slid over the circle and symbols etched into the varnished planks. Not just any circle. A magical one that my blood could activate. I'd killed a demon with it.

I think.

With no evidence of the death, I sometimes wondered if I'd dreamed it.

The house shivered. It didn't like it when I doubted. I could feel its frustration.

Then I was discomfited because you're not supposed to feel your house. Just like houses aren't supposed to widen stairs, add basements, or suddenly transform a shed into a garage. Yet my house did all that and more.

The town was right when it claimed my family were witches. Although I wasn't too sure if I counted given most of the magic I'd done came about by accident. I had no idea how I did stuff. There was no one to teach me except for an arrogant prick trying to get in my pants and an old book left to me by my grandma. I'd not had much time to read what with my new social life, job, and hobbies. Why care about magic when I had everything I needed?

Except apparently a doorbell. I opened the door, juggling one arm into my coat, hovering the coffee while the other arm sought out the sleeve. My left foot was halfway in my boot because something was stuffed in the toe. I didn't even notice the box.

I fell over it, smacking my chin, clacking my teeth, watering my eyes, but the biggest tragedy? My morning ambrosia. Gone. I almost cried at the loss.

"What the ever-loving fuck? Why put a package so close to the door?" My new potty mouth exclaimed before I could stop it.

"Mom! Language!" Poor Geoff sounded so shocked, and with good reason. Used to be I threatened his bad words with a bar of soap. Now, I could curse up a storm if I wanted.

It felt liberating and ironically cleansing.

"It's justified. That box almost killed me!" A slight exaggeration. The tree that fell on my car and the wolves hunting me had been slightly more perilous.

"I didn't hear anyone knock. They must have left it before I came upstairs."

It still blew my mind that I now had a basement level with a walkout. Before Geoff's arrival, I lived in a two-bedroom cozy cottage with my suite in the attic and Winnie in a small bedroom on the first floor.

Then my other child arrived, and a basement appeared with another bedroom, a full bathroom, and a rec area with a plaid couch, old fat television in a wooden base that probably needed four men to move, and a sliding glass door to a stone patio with a picnic table.

I didn't understand how that happened, but it was freaking cool. Made me wonder if I wished for a greenhouse or an arts and crafts room, what would happen?

I carried the box inside, not bothering to shut the door. The house did it for me. As I set it on the kitchen island, my kitty, Grisou, vaulted onto the granite top. It used to be butcher-block wood, but I really didn't like how the cat hair stuck to it. The house changed it. Just like the simple wooden cabinets, painted over a few times, now had a shaker style to them, and the sink was a deep farmhouse with a faucet pullout.

Ever since I'd bled on the house and started

believing, it was as if it thrived and sought to remake itself. I swear if one day I woke up in a castle, I'd probably piddle on the floor. And not because I sneezed too hard.

Geoff tried to shoo my cat from the counter. "Down."

"Leave him alone. He's fine." To me, Grisou was a member of my family who didn't deserve to live solely on the floor.

"It's not fine, Mom. It's gross. We eat here."

"And? It's just hair, Geoff." The words that came out of my mouth were so opposite to what I'd said to my kids growing up. I'd not put plastic on the couches, but it came close.

Grisou nosed the box as I read the label addressed to Mrs. Naomi Rousseaux. It came from some kind of legal office in the United States.

"What is it?" Geoff asked, drying his hands on a towel.

"I'm not sure." A frown pulled my features as I palmed a knife to slice at the tape.

As I pulled apart the cardboard flaps, Grisou let out a hiss then a low growl.

Even Geoff recoiled. "What's that smell?"

"Smells like something died." Looking inside the box, I saw a few things. Paper. Some clothing. Trinkets. A letter on top that started out, *Dear Mrs.*

Dunrobin, as the beneficiary of your late husband's estate…

I didn't close the flaps quick enough. Geoff saw, but rather than address it, he left the kitchen and returned to his cave. It didn't surprise me. He didn't talk about his father.

My very dead ex-husband.

Martin's body had been found on the other side of the lake. No one knew how he managed to escape jail then travel undetected from the States to Canada and the small town I now called home. The autopsy noted that he died of exposure caused by living in the woods as winter started.

Utter bullshit. Martin didn't have a single outdoorsy bone in his body. Not to mention, dying of the cold didn't explain the terror forever frozen on his face.

There was no sign of foul play. Officer Murphy couldn't pin it on me. I should have been ecstatic Martin was out of my life. That he could no longer follow through with his threats to kill me.

But something about the situation unsettled me.

With Geoff gone, I eyed the package. What use did I have for an ex-husband's things? I should toss it into the firepit out back and set it on fire.

Or should I hold on to it for Winnie or Geoff? While they weren't fond of their late father, they might eventually want something to remember him by.

Given Geoff's reaction, maybe I'd offer it to Winnie first. She'd hated him the least, and this in spite of how Martin treated her. Only as I held the package did I pause and second-guess my decision. What was inside?

What if it was full of porn magazines? A shiv? Maybe more of Martin's crazy manifesto that basically amounted to "kill that bitch." That bitch being me, of course. A smell still lingered around it. Death and something else. I wanted to say evil, but I didn't think it had a specific aroma.

"Meow."

My cat twined around my legs, a sinuous gray shape that had grown so much since I'd adopted his orphaned butt months ago.

"What do you think, Grisou?" I asked, shaking the package. "Maybe I should make sure there's nothing in there that might upset Winnie."

Better if it upset me. I could handle it.

Setting the box back on the counter, I started with the letter from the lawyer, a generic thing that basically amounted to the fact that Martin was dead and they didn't know who else to send his shit too. By the way, as his beneficiary in his will and testament, you'll have to settle his estate. In other words, find some money to pay their bill.

At that I snorted. Figured those vultures would want their piece.

I put the letter aside and pulled out the suit. His trial clothes that his lawyer arranged so he wouldn't appear in a prison jumpsuit.

In a manila envelope was his wallet with his identification and an invalid bank card. His reading glasses. Under that, evidence bags full of books. Notebooks both glue-spined and spiral bound. On the covers, dates. January 3rd, 2003 to August 14th, 2005.

Journals? Work ledgers? I was kind of curious. As I shifted the first bag, the smell erupted in all its rancid glory.

A glance within showed the culprit. A dead rodent. Barf. I didn't know how it got inside the box, but I knew it had to go.

I lifted my shirt over my nose and grabbed some tongs to lift the carcass out. Then, gagging and stomach heaving, ran for the back door. I didn't have shoes, so I did the responsible thing. I flung it. Mouse and tongs. With any luck, the critter would be dissolved by spring and I'd dispose of the tongs when I found them again.

I left the door open to remove the smell and headed back for the box. Curiosity filled me. I'd never known my husband kept any kind of journal. Where had he hidden them? In the garage where I rarely went? How did the lawyer get their hands on it? The evidence bags indicated the cops had confiscated the journals. Odd how I'd never heard of them when we went to court for his attempted murder of me. Then again, did they need more evidence? They had all they needed for a slam-dunk case.

Peering back inside the box, I snared the plastic sleeve that was marked with this year with no end date. He must have begun it in prison.

I pulled out the journal with its hard cover and flipped it open to see penned handwriting. Legible. An account of his life in prison.

Can't believe they arrested me. Can't they see what she is? She's dangerous. One of them. She took over my wife's body. She has to die.

2

IT CHILLED TO REALIZE HE SPOKE ABOUT ME. Slightly nauseous, I flipped deeper into the notebook and gagged in my shirt, not because the smell got worse but because of what I saw.

Scribbles and scribbles of something that had dried brown. Blood. He'd written in blood. Three words. Over and over. Sometimes only one word per page.

Kill that bitch.

I dropped the vile notebook. Definitely garbage. My kids didn't need to see their father's descent into madness. Perhaps he'd gotten some kind of brain parasite that chewed up his common sense.

Opening the cupboard under the sink, I prepared to dump it all, only to worry Winnie might see it and pull it out. Speaking of whom, she hustled through the door in a blast of cold air. Guilt made me shove box to the side, out of sight behind the counter.

"Morning, Winnie." Not her real name. That was actually Wendy. But I'd given her that nickname at a young age because she was my cuddly bear. "Late night?" She'd left not long after Darryl's visit.

"I spent the night with a friend." She practically glowed.

"Oh. Do I know them?"

"Yes. You do, and I don't need you getting judgy about it, which is why I'm not telling you who yet. I don't want to jinx it."

Would I get judgmental? Depended. Her last semi-boyfriend was much older than her and asked if I wanted to do a threesome with my daughter. The one before that was married and her college professor. She didn't have a great track record, but I'd learned what would happen if I told her I thought she was fucking up, so I stuck with, "I am so happy for you."

"Thanks, Mom." My girl grinned so wide she almost lost half her head. "I gotta go get ready for work. I start at ten and work until close. Don't wait up, though. I'm spending the night at my friend's house."

What should a mother say when confronted with her adult daughter being open about her sex life?

Old me might have spouted off something about giving away the cow, not respecting herself, or something judgmental and holier than thou. Why did I do that?

Why would I try to shame my daughter about being in charge of her body and sexuality?

I found the right reply. "Have fun and stay safe."

The big wide smile wrapped me in warmth. "I plan to have fun a few times." She winked.

I gasped. "Wendy Agatha Dunrobin."

She laughed, and a second later, I joined her.

I shook my head. "You're incorrigible."

"I know. One of my finer qualities. See ya tomorrow sometime." Winnie left, and still inwardly smiling, I started to make a new coffee. As I turned, I remembered the box on the floor.

Good thing Winnie hadn't seen it. If she'd asked, I don't know if I could have lied. Best hide it for now. I hefted the box and ran it to my bedroom, where I encountered the dilemma of where to put it. I crouched down and lifted the skirt on my bed mostly because it didn't have a skirt when I woke up. Look at that, enough space to tuck the box out of sight until I could burn it. At least the bad parts.

But before I could hide it, I needed to remove the Christmas presents under the bed. I pulled out the first box, flat and a large rectangle. The tag on it —in my writing despite me having never seen the present before—said, *To Geoff. Happy belated. Mom.*

Since I'd not expected his surprise visit for Christmas—and I mean surprise when I opened the door and my kid was standing there—I'd not bought anything. In my defense, I'd mailed a check which somehow ended up under the tree with an old pocket watch I'd never seen. so not entirely nothing, and yet, I felt horrible because his sister had so many gifts to open. My poor magical house, taken off guard, had nothing prepared. I wonder if it suffered anxiety at the thought.

Yes, magical house. I'd finally come to terms with the fact my home took care of me. From shifting subtly to match the house of my dreams to providing the things I needed. Like the smaller wrapped present, which I just knew was going to be some kind of game system.

"Thank you," I said aloud since I didn't know if my house could hear my thoughts or needed speech. Was it alive? Did it feel? Think?

I went with the flow and tried not to worry

about it, although I did wonder if some of the house's magic was bound in some way. Perhaps, complicated things like electronics were harder to create or acquire. Which begged the question, did my magical house actually perform replicator-type capabilities, or did it buy or steal what it needed?

My imagination conjured a cloud of minions, short and dressed uniformly with masks and slim-fitting unitards, piling out of some inter-dimensional rip. They'd scurry to take what they needed and pop back through a portal.

It would be cool if true.

Eyeing the large present—apparently the house really wanted to make an impression—I said, "I don't suppose you could deliver them to the basement?"

I would have sworn I felt an answering hum. The presents went back under the bed, and I grabbed Martin's box, meaning to do the same.

As I went to shift it, it tilted over, and some bags slid out. The topmost one had neat and tidy writing. The date? The year I met Martin. He'd kept a journal while we were dating? Did I know my husband of more than two decades at all?

On a whim, I grabbed the notebook and sat on the window seat, feet tucked up as I read. Him getting to college. His room. His classes. Then…

Met a cute girl today. Think I'll ask her out.

Looking at the date, I could only surmise I was the girl.

I kept reading.

There's something special about Naomi. And tragic too. Horrible that she lost her parents. Makes me wish I had a family to give her.

As I kept reading, nostalgia for the man that once loved me filled me. Nice to know I'd not imagined we were once in love. What I didn't understand was what happened to change it? How had we gone from a young couple taking on the world as a team to tiptoeing around each other? Then keep moving to the hate Martin exhibited at the end. I eyed the journals, the smell not as bad now that I'd taken them out of the box. Maybe I shouldn't burn them quite yet.

Could I find out where things went wrong? Did I even want to know?

Honestly? Maybe. But not today.

Piling the stuff back in the box, I slid it out of sight. For a second, I wondered if the house would take care of it for me.

Having gone from being on time to running behind, I barely had time to whip together a bulletproof coffee. As a low-carb convert, I fasted in the morning, drinking a coffee laced with MCT oil and a dash of cream frothed together. It would keep me going until lunch.

As I drove toward town, I passed the gas station and glanced over to see if I could spot Darryl's truck. He wasn't in yet, although I'd probably see him at one point. Since Christmas he'd made a point of seeing me, even if briefly, every day. Like Boxing Day when he'd shown up to eat leftovers with me. Apparently, the man loved turkey.

Wendy and Geoff had gone to town looking for deals, so it was just him and me. He'd kissed me after that meal. A simple kiss that ended too soon for me. I was hungry.

An odd word to use but true. I'd wanted to do so much more with Darryl. Wanted to climb between some sheets naked and go to town.

It was embarrassing and hot at the same time. If only his phone hadn't gone off. Emergency at the gas station.

He'd had to leave.

I'd seen him to the door then practically raced to my room, where I masturbated twice, thinking about him. Shocking and fun. I'd not had that many orgasms in years. Decades even. Had I finally entered my sexual peak? I really shouldn't waste it.

Maybe on my lunch break I'd pop over to see Darryl. This was, after all, not the eighties and nineties anymore. A woman didn't have to wait for a man to make the moves.

And I was ready to move. It had been years since I'd had sex. My now-dead husband had lost interest. In me at any rate. Apparently, he had no problem with his girlfriend.

Ugh. It was a kick to the teeth. But I was stronger now. Desired by a handsome man. I needed to carve some alone time for him.

I parked in the alley behind my shop, leaving the on-street spaces for shoppers. Of late, it seemed there were more and more people in town. Signs of life were everywhere. A steady flow of cars rolled up and down the main street. The café where I used to work, Maddy's Family Diner, busted at the seams. It was so busy that Orville, the owner, had to hire a few more waitresses to help out. Marjorie, who still worked there, said the tips had never been better. What no one seemed to question was where all these strangers came from. They took over the houses and businesses bought up by the huge giant of a company, Airgeadsféar. They'd even tried to buy my grandma's cottage. I'd refused, and then I'd snatched up a shop from under them. Yay for me.

It appeared to be a sound investment, as the dusty town found itself revived by the newly repurposed mill. I profited. Before Christmas, a steady stream of people discovered my eclectic wares. Antiques and oddities, some of the goodies I sold I'd found scattered around my cottage, making me wonder how long the house could keep coughing up antiques. Other items I sold on consignment for Darryl. Did he really need to clean out his house, or was it an excuse to see me?

Maybe a bit of both. But I had to keep in mind the steady flow of merchandise wouldn't last. I needed other sources. On my list was attending estate sales and auctions to widen my offerings and have a legal paper trail in case I got audited.

As I entered from the back, I flipped on switches. The filtered daylight didn't take away all the gloom. I walked right to the front and unlocked the store, getting a strange satisfaction in flipping the sign from closed to open. A peek onto the street showed the bookstore across from me already had its sign on the sidewalk announcing a BOGO—buy one get one—on all their books. The flower shop adjacent had colorful arrangements in the window and was already serving customers. Those walking the sidewalk seemed undaunted by the chill of winter. It was a like a throwback to the images of the perfect town in the 1950s.

Some of that traffic came to see me. I sold enough that morning to ensure the electricity got paid for the next month. Around lunchtime, I got hungry. I had a sign for that, too. Out for lunch, back by one. The one being chalked in by me.

Just as I was about lock up and track down Darryl, the door opened, and a woman entered. She was older than me, I'd wager, with her paper-thin skin and wrinkles tugging parts of her face. Elegant, with her hair pulled back, makeup perfect from her lightly pink cheeks to subtle eye shadow and mascara. Perfectly dressed, her pencil skirt past her knees and a somber gray. Her jacket tightly tailored and threaded with some mauve. It matched the frothy lace emerging from her neckline.

Guess I'd be delaying my lunch—and possible kisses with Darryl—for a few more minutes. "Hello and welcome to On My Way."

The icy gaze took me in. Up. Down. Disdain clear as she said, "So you're the whore dabbling with my son."

3

As statements went, that caught my attention.

"Excuse me? I think you must be mistaken." Because I was pretty sure whores had sex. Lots of it. And I didn't think masturbation counted.

"I hope I'm mistaken. He usually has better taste." Her lips curved into a cruel smirk.

Ouch. The insult stung. Especially after everything I'd done to lose weight and regain my sense of self. "I think you should leave. You are obviously in the wrong place."

"I was told this is where the slut works."

Uh-oh. I suddenly had a sinking feeling. Was this about Winnie and her new friend? "That is really harsh language to use." Please don't tell me I'd ever been this nasty.

"Only if it were false. I'm here to put a stop to it."

"Or maybe you shouldn't interfere? When kids reach a certain age, we have to let them make their own choices."

"He was told to stay away."

"What can I say? Young love." I shrugged.

She snorted. "He's old enough to know better. But since he's incapable of breaking it off, I'll handle it for him."

From the sounds of it, Winnie was better off not getting involved with this family. Mommy was whack-a-doodle. "I'll pass on the message."

"I'll do it myself. Where is Naomi Rousseau? I hear she's the owner of this store."

I blinked. It only briefly occurred to me to lie. "I'm Naomi."

"The whore?"

"Doubtful. I haven't had sex in… Doesn't matter how long. Let's just say if your son claimed he was sleeping with me, then he was lying."

"I know you're involved with him, whore."

I cleared my throat. "Would you mind not calling me that? I wasn't kidding when I said I've been celibate for years. Unless battery operated counts." I said it, and I couldn't take it back.

The lady in front of me only got meaner. "Are

you going to deny you've been distracting my son? Plying your wiles on him. Making him forget his familial obligations."

It couldn't be Darryl she was talking about. His parents weren't around. Who did that leave? "Who the hell are you talking about?"

"Don't play stupid. My son Kane."

"You think Kane and I are fooling around?" I blurted out then laughed. "Hell no." Not because the guy was ugly or gross. I'd had a one-night make-out session with Kane. I was drunk. Desperate. We made out. It was hot. Very hot. Also all kinds of wrong since Kane was more interested in my property than me. Good thing my bestie saved me from making a mistake.

A mistake that wanted to repeat itself. Kane kept coming around. Not because I asked him too. He just appeared at random moments, mostly to drive me wild, but the last time I'd seen him, he saved my life, and since then he'd avoided me.

Totally for the best because I was serious about Darryl. I liked him a lot and wouldn't do anything to wreck my chances with him.

"Don't deny you've done something to my son," exclaimed Kane's mom. "You cast a spell. Ensnared him with your wiles."

It was so ludicrous I couldn't stop laughing. "Oh

my God. You are seriously crazy. Talk to Kane. He'll tell you there's nothing going on between us."

"But that would be a lie, sweetheart," the devil himself said as he walked into the store, interjecting himself into the conversation as if he'd been listening. Then again, he probably had been.

I scanned Kane for injury, because the last time I'd seen him, he was confronting a pack of wolves, injured and alone with only a sword. Defending me. The only thing that would have made it hotter was if he'd taken off his shirt.

Then I remembered I was annoyed with him, mostly because he'd not contacted me once to let me know he was okay. I'd even caved and sent him a message to which he never replied, which hurt. Then made me mad because I cared, and I didn't want to.

"What do you want?" I snapped. "Can't you see I'm having a lovely chat with your mother?" I was heavy on the sarcasm. Maybe they'd get the hint and both leave.

"A chat about me, I assume. Surely you don't mind if I join in."

"Actually, I do mind," I huffed, my indignation only partially authentic. Kane might be a tad older than Darryl, the lines in his face more severe, rigid, but there was something about him. A masculinity. A presence. Danger that thrilled.

"I understand you're angry. It's been a few days without contact. You must have missed me."

He did this all the time. Spoke as if we had something between us. Disturbing and sexy at the same time. Why couldn't I just hate him? How could I be attracted? I was involved with Darryl.

"I hadn't even noticed." A lie. I'd checked my phone more than a few times to see if he'd called or texted a reply. A perverse part of me wanted to see if he'd try and reach out so I could smack him down.

His mother launched into some speech in a language I couldn't hope to follow, and Kane replied, "Say it in English so Naomi can understand."

"You agreed you'd stay away from her," hissed his mommy.

"Wouldn't be the first time I went back on my word."

His own statement proved he was bad, so why did I tingle?

"There is too much at stake for you to be doing this," his mother insisted.

"And you are overstepping," was his reply.

"I will when you are making such a grave mistake." Mommy dearest wasn't letting up.

Kane only got more amused, and I finely understood the term supercilious smile. "I will see Naomi if I choose, and you will mind your business about it."

My turn to have a say. "No, you will not see me. I am not interested in anything involving you." A lie that ignored my racing pulse.

"Are you sure about that? As I recall, at our last meeting, there remained unresolved issues."

Way to remind me. I didn't just have questions about why Kane walked around with a sword. He knew about magic and monsters, like the one that attacked us in the woods. He had answers. I just didn't know if I could trust him—or myself. My feelings for Kane kept surprising me, mostly because I had some.

"If I wanted your help I would ask." Left unsaid? I thought about it a few times. I hung up before the phone rang each time. Deleted every text after the first one I sent. I didn't want to appear desperate.

"It's not as if he could have answered, given his injuries." It was his mother who exposed him.

"How badly were you hurt?" I couldn't help the blurted concern.

"I'm fine," he said tightly.

"You're not fine. You shouldn't even be out of bed." His mother again spilled more than he wanted to reveal, judging by his expression.

"Would you keep your mouth shut," he growled. "I wouldn't have had to leave bed if you'd not taken it upon yourself to meddle in affairs that are none of your business." His anger vibrated in his tone and posture.

"She's blinding you to your duty."

"My duty? You are not in the position to lecture me about duty," he snarled right back.

Her lips pinched. "You will regret your actions. Mark my words. They won't be forgotten." With that, she swept out of my store.

And my smart-ass mouth said, "Wow, I bet family dinners are just a blast at your place."

4

"WHY DON'T YOU JOIN ME AT THE NEXT FAMILY dinner to find out?" Kane always had a smooth reply.

"I'm good, thanks. Although you have my condolences. Growing up must have been tons of fun." With Kane's mother gone, it left us alone. Me and Kane with only a few feet between us. I already knew he wasn't the type who believed in social distancing, despite the fact it trended for years after the pandemic. I'd need to get rid of him quick.

"While you might not have seen it, I assure you my mother has my best interests at heart. Mostly because it serves her agenda."

"What kind of agenda says it's okay to visit a stranger and call her…" I couldn't say it and settled for, "A bad name?"

"I'm sorry she confronted you. It's why I followed her the moment I heard."

And his mother gave him shit for that, too. I eyed him. "How badly are you still hurt?" And why did I feel guilty I'd not checked in on him? The man saved my life. He didn't answer one text and I'd assumed he'd been ignoring me instead of considering the possibility he couldn't respond.

"I'll live."

"That's not an answer. Where were you hurt?"

"Is this your less-than-subtle attempt to remove my clothing? You know, all you have to do is ask." He practically purred the words.

I was tempted. Curious. What did he look like under those layers? Today he wore a dark bomber jacket over an open-necked button shirt tucked into jeans. It was the most casual I'd seen him. His hair wasn't as perfect as usual. The lines on his face spoke of fatigue.

I should send him home, and yet, I had questions. "What's going on in this town?"

"I would have said tons of development. The place is busy since I last popped in."

"Because of the mill. But that's not the only thing. There's something else going on. I know it."

"Whatever do you mean?"

I glared. "Don't pull that bullshit with me."

Look at me, getting all tough. "I don't know if it's the lake, the town, or some ancient burial ground, but there is weird shit happening. And you're right in the middle of it. You and that mill." I still remembered my first visit to it and seeing the mechanical monster that mined the bottom of the lake. The odd mining machine made a plausible explanation for monster sightings. That night, I had my first Maddy dream. More like a nightmare.

At first, I feared Maddy because she would always devour me. But as the dreams evolved, the swallowing me whole stopped, and I got to see a monster in great pain. A creature suffering. A prisoner slowly dying.

"Funny you should ask about the mill. Operations there are wrapping up."

"So quickly?" It didn't make sense. The launch was for the new year. Now, I didn't know much about business, but shouldn't the production be ongoing?

"Doesn't feel quick to me. Once upon a time it took forever to reach this point. Now? We are almost at the end."

"The end of what?"

I expected another bullshit answer, but he offered a bleak reply. "The end of a long effort. An era. A life."

He spoke of life, and on an impulse, I asked, "Did Maddy die? Is that why you can't keep the mill open?"

His brows rose. "What makes you think she died?"

"I saw it in a dream." I admitted it to the only person I could.

His chin dropped. "Have you seen other things?" He didn't mock me.

I shook my head. "Nothing I really remember or understand other than Maddy, and in my last one, she wasn't there. Just the lake and beach."

"She's gone." He confirmed it and wavered on his feet. He didn't look well.

"You should sit down. Or better yet, go home. To bed." My questions could wait until he recovered.

"Will you join me?"

I ignored the tingles. This insane attraction was just more proof I needed to get laid. Maybe then everything with a penis wouldn't make me horny. "Why do you keep pretending we have a thing? I'm not interested."

"So you keep saying."

"If you hear me, then why are you ignoring me?"

"Because it amuses me to make you angry." He smirked.

"And does it amuse you to piss off your mom, too? Why make her believe that we are involved?"

"Because we are, if not perhaps in the way I'd like or that you expect."

"That is a load of baloney."

"Are you claiming you feel nothing?" He stepped closer to the counter, and my heart raced so fast I worried he'd notice.

"I'm seeing someone."

"You may want to rethink your interest in Darryl. He's using you."

"That's ridiculous. I have nothing he wants."

"Don't you? He needs you."

"And how is that a bad thing?" I could think of worse things than having a man want and need me. I ignored the little voice that had naughty suggestions as to what Darryl *really* wanted.

"Because he—"

Ding a ling. The door to my shop rang, and Darryl walked in.

Hot guilt and giddy relief filled me as I exclaimed, "Darryl! I was just about to close shop and go find you." I held up a sign.

"Were you really?" There was suspicion in his tone as he glanced at Kane standing close to me.

"Kane was just leaving," I announced.

"Is he?" Darryl drawled. "I'm surprised to see you here, *Kane*." He put an odd inflection on the name. "I heard you suffered a mishap."

How come Darryl knew of Kane's injuries but I didn't?

Kane shrugged. "Grossly exaggerated. Feeling fine and thought I'd get out."

"Glad to hear it," Darryl said as he stepped close enough to slap Kane on the back.

The wince came and went quick enough that I wondered if I'd imagined it.

"Go back to bed," I said. "I don't think you're well enough to be out and about."

Kane didn't argue. "You know how to reach me if you need me."

"She won't need you. She has me," was Darryl's caveman assertion. Sexy, with a hint of violence. I'd never seen Darryl other than affable. Could he be jealous?

Of moi? A girly thrill ran through me. It turned into pure pleasure as Darryl got close enough to slide his arm loosely around my waist.

I'd just been claimed. And my panties weren't wet because I peed myself.

With a rigid expression, Kane left, and I

quashed my irrational guilt. I had nothing to feel bad about. On the contrary…

"I'm so happy to see you," I said, pivoting to smile up at Darryl.

"Are you?"

Oh, my sweet baby Jeezus, he *was* jealous. I gave him a quick peck. "Very."

Still he scowled. "I don't like him coming around."

"It's not like I had a choice. He just showed up." Was it wrong to be thrilled at his macho demands?

"I'll deal with him."

A frown pulled my brow. "What's that mean? You're not going to fight him, are you?"

"Worried about him?"

"More like I don't want to see you get in trouble. I'm not interested in Kane." I cupped Darryl's face. "Why would I when I have you?"

The statement pleased him. He smiled. "Were you really coming to find me?"

I nodded. "I thought we could do lunch."

"Wish I could, but I'm going to be busy today. I've got family stuff to deal with again."

"Is everything okay?" He'd been handling a few emergencies of late. Made me wonder what kind of crisis kept cropping up and why he had to deal with it. After all, his parents and grandparents weren't around. I'd not heard of any siblings. Who did that leave, and why were they so important to him?

"It will be soon. Until then, I might not be around too much."

"Oh." Yeah, that was a bit of a sad sound.

"That doesn't mean you won't see me." He gave me a squeeze.

"I'm glad." Then before I lost the courage, said, "What are you doing New Year's?"

"Spending it with you, of course."

The unexpected answer flustered me, and he took that opportunity to kiss me. Softly. A gentle sliding of his mouth over mine. His hands squeezed my ass.

The fire between my legs throbbed. Needed.

So I was more than disappointed when he pulled away. "Wish I had time to finish this, but I have to go."

Being desperate, I almost asked him for two more minutes. I was pretty sure I could get what I needed that quick. However, I'd used up my bravery quotient with my half-assed New Year's Eve demand.

With one last kiss, Darryl left. After a few minutes of staring into space, I put the sign in the window and went into the back. I didn't need batteries, not with knowing fingers. I came quick.

After washing my hands, I popped out to grab a salad from the new healthy-option bistro two shops down from me.

It almost felt disrespectful to Orville, who, in the past, had made me all kinds of special treats. However, I wasn't ready to be around my friends right after an orgasm. I just wanted to eat my avocado chicken salad in peace and bask in my happiness.

The afternoon went quickly, with no visits from anyone I knew. At five-ish I got a text from Trish saying, *We still on?*

Hell yeah. Good food and girl gab? I'd gone almost twenty years without having a close friend. I wasn't letting my bestie go for anything.

Despite it being busy, we met at Maddy's Family Diner. Marjorie kept a booth reserved for us. She hustled up to it, slapping the menus on the table before turning to Trish. "I might not have time to join you."

"Thanks for keeping us a spot," Trish said to Marjorie as she dropped a kiss on her lips. They'd finally decided to stop hiding they were a couple. I could only hope no one was a jerk about it. I'd hex them if they said anything.

"The place is packed," I remarked.

"Hasn't stopped all day. I had to come in at noon instead of three to help out."

"You working until what time?" Trish asked.

"Orville says we're to close the kitchen at eight, everyone out by nine."

Orville being the burly owner. Super nice man. If I weren't dating Darryl, I might have been interested.

"Is Orville working tonight? I don't see him." I glanced over in the direction of the kitchen.

"The man is actually taking the evenings off. He hired two cooks to handle the dinner shift."

"Wow." I was surprised given the diner was his baby. Then again, given the brisk business, a break was well deserved.

"I think he met someone," Marjorie confided.

Shy Orville? I had a hard time imagining it. He was a gentle giant. Gruff, yet soft spoken with a heart of gold, always insisting on walking me to my car the days I came for dinner alone.

Marjorie left with our orders, and Trish jumped right to it. "Rumor has it you had a visit from Kane and his mom."

"How did you know?" I still hadn't quite gotten used to how quickly news moved in a small town.

"Someone saw her car parked outside your shop. What did she want?"

"To warn me off of her son," I said with a laugh. "She thinks Kane and I have a thing going on."

"Do you?"

"No!"

"Protesting much?" Trish arched a brow. She'd tamed her hair for work, pulling it back in a bushy pony wrapped in a bright strip of cloth that matched the hue of her shirt.

"I do not have a thing for Kane."

It was over eggplant lasagna, with ground beef, mushrooms, and tons of cheese, that I managed to mumble, "Any recommendations on where I can buy some cute underwear? I think I'm ready to get rid of my granny panties." Comfortable to the extreme, up to my waist, cotton, loose. But not exactly the sexiest thing.

My BFF didn't bat an eye as she said, "The kind that is cute but functional, or that screams, take me, I'm yours?"

"Both?"

"Things must be getting serious between you and Darryl." Trish nodded with approval. She'd been team Darryl from the start.

"I think so. He came by the store today just to say hi."

"Only hi?"

I blushed. "We're taking things slow." Mostly by circumstance. I was ready to ignore my previous trepidation and go for it.

"Slow can be nice," she said. "Although I expected that more of Jace than him."

She referred to my reticent neighbor, who lately appeared to be keeping to himself. The brief occasions I'd seen him, he'd been skulking in the shadows, dragging around that axe of his. I used to wonder why until I met some of the monsters that lived in the forest around Cambden.

"What are you two chatting about?" Marjorie arrived with coffee and slid into the booth beside Trish.

"Darryl popped in to say hi to Naomi today."

"Oh, how cute. You and Darryl are adorbs," she declared.

"Thanks." We did have a lot in common being just normal, blue-collar folk. About the same age. We both knew the words to eighties music. I flashed for a second to Kane. Slightly older, a jet-setting architect who'd been pictured intimately with models. I'd never be able to compete.

Wait, why would I want to? Kane and I were nothing. I had Darryl. A guy I was over the moon for.

"So when are you planning for Darryl to see

your underwear?" Marjorie asked, and I spewed coffee.

Choked for a good minute while Trish killed herself laughing.

"Not funny," I managed to complain in a raspy voice. "Almost drowned."

"If you'd seen the look of panic on your face." Trish snickered.

"Don't tease her too bad. It's not easy getting your feet wet after a bad relationship," Marjorie, whom we sometimes called Jojo, chided.

"She's got to get on that horse sooner or later," Trish remarked.

"I will. I am. Soon." Should I tell them he planned to spend New Year's with me? Hopefully I wouldn't chicken out. Having nice panties was all well and good, but I also had to show him the rest of me. Stretch marks. Loose skin. A history etched on my flesh. I wasn't a woman in her twenties but one creeping up on fifty.

Life left its mark. Surely Darryl would understand. After all, when I first met him, he'd been a bit overweight and unkempt, too. I liked to think his attention to his appearance started because of me.

"Soon means we need to get it done."

"I'm not working tomorrow," Marjorie stated.

"Since it's Friday, I can close the municipal

office early. It's not like people are stampeding for town services right now." Trish worked as a clerk handing out permits and information.

"I'm surprised you're not busy. Seems like the town is crowded lately." A glance around the diner showed it packed. The faces all new to me.

"Lots of new folk moving in, plus we got a few that showed up to be a part of the New Year's Eve event."

"What event?"

Marjorie blinked her heavily mascaraed eyes at me. "How have you not heard about it? The one at the mill. *The* party?"

I shook my head.

"The mill is throwing a New Year's Eve bash. Catered food. Drinks. And the whole town is invited."

"I already have plans to spend it with Darryl."

"Doing what?"

I'd actually not thought that far ahead. "I don't know." Other than I'd assumed it would involve sex at one point.

"You're going to the party," Marjorie declared.

"I should talk to Darryl first."

"He's probably assuming it's a foregone conclusion." Trish tag-teamed with her girlfriend. She did technically know him better than me.

"Okay. I guess we're going to the mill."

"Do you have an evening gown?" Marjorie asked.

Trish snorted. "I've seen her closet. She'll need a dress along with the lingerie."

Marjorie clapped her hands. "This is sounding to me like a girls' day at the mall that ends in dinner."

It did, and it delighted me to be a part of it. "Sounds like a plan. Say midafternoon tomorrow?"

"Yes. And be sure to invite Winnie."

"I will." Although, given her new friend, I had my doubts she'd come.

As for Geoff, I hoped he'd understand. At least he had the Christmas gift he could play now. Although I did wonder how long he planned to stay. He'd arrived Christmas Eve and had yet to tell me when he planned to return home. I didn't dare ask, mostly because it seemed odd he hadn't spent the holidays with his fiancée. As a matter of fact, other than stating she had to work for the holidays, he'd not mentioned Helena to me once. Had something happened?

I wanted to ask, but I chickened out. For me, it was enough Geoff had sought me out. We'd not had the best relationship in the last decade or so, but I was ready to start over.

Finished with dinner, I left my friends with a wave and promises to meet by the ice cream place in the mall the next day at three. Since Orville wasn't at work, I had to walk by myself to the alley by my shop. Once I'd have been a nervous wreck, with fingers white-knuckled around my car keys. I had this belief that danger lurked in every shadow. That bad things would befall me.

That was the old, scared Naomi.

Now, my head remained high, my gaze steady, and my nerves calm. I'd faced many challenges of late. Some of them deadly. And you know what? I'd come through them all. Even fought back in some cases. I wasn't weak or cowardly.

It made me think of a meme I'd seen about a woman entering her don't-give-a-fuck forties. That was me. I'd survived so much. I could handle anything.

Even a dark alley. An alley that got darker the more steps I took. My anxiety tickled inside me. Trepidation prickled my skin. The air frosted, my breath white puffs of steam. My lashes iced.

This wasn't the first time an uncanny chilliness came after me, but I'd been studying the sigils in my house and online. Identifying the magic hexes used to defend and in some cases attack. I also travelled armed with chalk just in case I needed to use my new knowledge.

I knelt on the ground, a piece of chalk in hand. Not that I'd need it with frost limning the asphalt. Perfect for drawing. I traced in it, doing my best to ignore the ominous creeping presence—until it made a noise!

The scrabble of feet momentarily distracted and a quick glance showed several sets of eyes glinting at me. High. Low. Ominous.

I finished drawing the symbol and felt it fluttering to life when I placed my hand on it. It wanted to act. It just needed a little more motivation. I spit on it. Blood would be more potent, according to my internet research; however, I wasn't keen on cutting myself every time I wanted to use magic.

Bodily fluids. That was what the marks demanded because it somehow linked a witch to the magic. At the combination, the sigil flared, its shape giving it a direction and purpose, only needing a push from me to complete it.

I whispered intent into the spell. "Give me some light."

Brightness oozed from the mark to dispel the darkness. The eyes fled, uttering keening cries that receded. All the shadows burned away. I squinted and closed my lids against it. Too bright. Too fucking bright.

Where was the switch to turn it off?

Poof. That suddenly, the light went out. The bulbs reignited as electricity was restored. The frost faded. The faceless and nameless evil that kept coming after me was gone. I still didn't understand why it attacked, but finally, I knew how to fight.

I stood and smiled. Maybe I could get the hang of this witch thing. But I drew the line at riding a broom.

5

My car, which was a perfect-condition Hyundai Pony, chugged as I headed home. Navy blue vinyl seats matched the dash. The exterior was a cream color. There were four doors with roll-down windows and no AC.

Be jealous of my vintage ride—unless it was stinking hot in the summer. I remembered my grandma always putting a towel down on the seat so I wouldn't burn myself on hot plastic. Vinyl proved to be easy to clean but horrible for comfort. Maybe I'd get some car seat covers. A present to myself to celebrate my magical victory. I'd flouted The Chill without anyone's help, not Jace or my house, nor did Kane ride to my rescue.

I could defend myself. The knowledge made me

eager to learn more. What did the marks in my house mean? They were etched all over: windowsills, doors, the beams that formed the roof in the attic. My grandma's old recipe book used to have them too, but the darned thing had disappeared on me again. I had it in my car, and now it was gone. Book snatched!

Good thing I had a few pictures stored on my phone. Zooming brought forth some examples. I did a reverse image search on the squiggly sigil I used this very night, the one for light, and I found a forum dedicated to witches and sorceresses. Warlocks, too, but they, for the most part, appeared to be rather pompous asses.

I devoured the thread on my light sigil. People actually discussing how the magic of it worked. They were frank about their successes. Chalk was good, as it wrote on most surfaces. Liquid could run and distort lines, making the sigil a dud. They even discussed how the curvature on it would strengthen or diminish the amount of brightness. Like a switch. Good to know for next time.

Because there would be another attack either by The Chill or more winged minions of darkness. Since my arrival, the feints against me had been constant. They'd also failed, and now I found myself suddenly pumped by the idea of not waiting for them to come after me. I should hunt the evil down.

How dare it keep attacking. What had I done to it? My faceless enemy owed me an explanation, maybe an apology, and then I'd hex their ass. There was a mark to do it. Supposedly it gave the hexed a hairy, boil-covered butt.

But taking down my enemies in cruel ways wasn't the only thing I studied. I avidly followed a discussion started by the KingofKnaves69, which itemized the various fluids that could be used to access magic, blood being the most powerful of what they called the necro magic. That was followed by spit then urine. Even cum, both male ejaculate and female fluid, could pack a punch, making orgies especially potent.

I preferred to cut myself rather than become the filling in a sex sandwich. I was more of a one-person-at-a-time kind of gal. So sex magic was out. Nor did I ever see myself using menstrual blood. Used tampons belonged in the garbage, not to mention there was an argument that the unfertilized lining had adverse effects on spells, while others said the raw potential in it added a richness.

All the witches agreed that amniotic fluid trumped all, with men unable to tap it. The fluid could only be used by the mother.

But that wasn't the case with blood. A witch could sacrifice someone else for the more powerful stuff. Apparently, a witch gang—known as the Baker's Coven—bragged about how they only used the blood of their enemies for their spells.

Fucking witch gangs. I wondered if they got to wear cute jackets and went on cruises.

As I drove, I thought about the other things I'd learned, such as that the gene for magic was hereditary, more often passed on via the female branches. Knowing my grandma had powers, I now was curious. Did my mother have magic, too? As for my dad, he must have known, and yet he never told me. He moved me far away from my grandma when I was a young girl. By the time I returned after his death, my eyes and ears were closed to the truth.

Not anymore. *I am special.* And I wanted to know what it meant. Such as, did my kids carry the witchy blood, too? After all they were both mine. Mine, but one of them wasn't Martin's, according to my grandma's book. I'd inherited the genealogy book from her. The leather on it was smooth, the tree etched on the cover a prelude to what was inside.

I'd finally figured out how to read it. It contained the names of my ancestors. Pages of them, going back centuries, branching in ways that boggled the mind. It took flipping to the very rear and the last few empty spots to find the lineage I was looking for. The Rousseaux family. I traced the names with my finger, recognizing those of my great-grandparents, who had two children. Their son died without heirs, leaving my grandma, who'd had two daughters. The oldest died young. My poor grandmother, outliving both her children. My mom had only me. I popped out two babies.

Geoff first, with the line for father oddly blank, and then my daughter with a name filled in under father that I didn't recognize.

Even now, the recollection of what I'd seen in that book had me tightening my hands on the wheel. White-knuckling it. Stressed, too. A part of me wanted to forget what I'd seen. Obviously, the person who'd written it in was mistaken.

I didn't know a Berith. And who had only one name?

A lie. At the same time, I couldn't ignore it. After all, Grandma was a witch. She knew things, and many of those things were in the books I'd inherited. There were three of them in total, differing in appearance and content. One a book of kitchen remedies passed down, essentially a grimoire of spells that could be whipped up at home—although I was having trouble collecting tears of joy from a murderer.

The second book contained the Rousseaux family tree.

To round it out was a third creepy book, bound by some strap and unwilling to open. It made me wonder what was inside.

I mean look at what I'd discovered in the lineage book. So many stories of my ancestors, male and female alike. Some generations needing only a paragraph to summarize their accomplishments, others taking pages. The writing was tight, faded, and in a language I couldn't read until the entries of about a century ago.

My great-great-grandmother had a short passage where I'd gleaned she considered herself the guardian of Cambden, and especially of the lake. What the summary didn't explain was what she guarded and why, only that she took the task seriously. One of her daughters, great-aunt Mathilda, died young but managed a line that said, *Died to fulfill the terms of the pact.*

What pact?

My grandmother was the only person of her generation to stay in Cambden. All her siblings and cousins left. Their lines died out. My grandmother had an empty spot where her life summary would have gone. My mother's section had a few shaky lines done in handwriting I recognized. My grandmother had left some words.

May she find peace in the next life.

Even my dad had something for his. *He should have known fate would drag her back.*

My gaze kept going back to Grandma's blank summary. Who was supposed to write it? Her children were long gone, and I never realized my grandmother was a witch. I'd been so blind to everything until I came home.

But more disturbing than the blank spots for Grandmother and the cryptic messages for my parents was the fact I knew who wrote in the wrong name for Winnie's father. I knew that handwriting. Very neat despite its cursive whorls. Impossible. My grandmother died before either of the children was born.

Obviously, the book worked off some kind of magic. It didn't mean it was true. The claim was crazy. I'd never cheated on my husband. Never even thought of it

Yet this book had the name Berith inscribed. I wondered... Flipping back through the pages, the generations, I noticed no other incidents of the sort except for a great-great-great-something aunt, who had a different father for each of her kids. But those men all had proper names.

The book obviously got the wrong information. But who would have lied to it?

Thinking about that stupid book made me miss the entrance to my driveway. It meant turning around at the next house. As I pulled in so that I could turn around, I noticed my neighbor had the curtains on his place drawn tight. Usually Jace skulked around the woods, a master at spooking me. Him and his axe. For a short while, I'd thought him interested in me given how often he appeared when I was in trouble, a hero to save me. But of late, he was nowhere to be seen. It was like he'd disappeared and along with him the constant suggestions I leave and never come back.

I reversed and managed to find the right driveway. Look at me, I arrived home intact. No tree falling on my car. No sudden slick roads and spooky shit sending me spinning into ditches. All hail Naomi, conquering the commute.

I parked by my garage, with carriage house doors that I freaking loved, and eyed the expansive window on the second story. New since this morning.

Please let it be a studio. I'd discovered a love of art. Not a skill, I should add. My attempts were atrocious in most cases, and yet that didn't stop me from wanting to create.

I entered the house, and the only one to greet me was my cat. With a strident meow, Grisou came running out of nowhere and slammed into my legs. He'd gotten awfully big. Winnie joked I'd adopted a Maine Coon, which apparently got to be huge.

Whatever the case, my kitten wasn't easy to grab and snuggle anymore, but he kept me warm at night when he slept on my bed.

I scratched Grisou behind the ears, and his aircraft carrier rumble brought a smile. "I missed you, too. Maybe next week you can come to the shop with me. See if there's any mice."

My cat cocked his head as if thinking about it then sauntered off, tail in the air. His version of "I'll let you know at my convenience." His attitude made me understand all the cat memes I'd seen over the years. They truly were feline gods.

I knocked on the basement door and waited for a shout to go down a flight. Geoff was parked on the couch in front of his new gaming center.

He cast me a quick glance. "Hey, Mom."

"Hey right back at you. I just got home."

"You looking for some company?" He paused the game.

Just as I was about to say yeah, that would be

awesome, his phone rang. He grabbed it and glanced at the screen.

He sighed. "It's Helena. I'll call her back."

Helena his fiancée? "You should answer. I'm tired and going to bed. I'll see you in the morning. Say hi for me."

"Will do. Love ya."

It was casual, but I soaked it up as I headed upstairs to the main floor then another flight to my room. There was a time I would have huffed and puffed. Now, I was just energized.

A bath would be nice, but I hesitated. The last time I took a bath, my home was invaded by winged imps and a giant demon that wanted to fight.

And ignorant little me won. I'd won without any kind of knowledge or skill, and I knew more now. I wouldn't let fear control me.

I ran the bath and went looking for reading material. The family tree book taunted, but I feared getting annoyed enough that I'd intentionally drop it in the tub to ruin it. I found myself instead scrounging under the bed and pulling out Martin's box. I dragged it into the open and scrounged inside for the journals, eyeing the dates. The one I grabbed covered the year before Winnie's birth.

Martin was her dad. The journal would confirm it.

I took the thick, hard-covered book into the bathroom and set it on a stool by the tub, along with my phone just in case the crazy was too much and I wanted to play Candy Crush. It was relaxing to the extreme.

I stepped into the tub and had a sighing moment as the heat relaxed me. My eyes shut, and I reflected on my day, which—other than the visit from Kane's mom—was a good one. Even the bit in the alley where I protected myself had been good. I'd come a long way from the woman contemplating suicide when her husband dumped her.

And I was still only halfway there. I had another possible forty to fifty years to go. To learn. To grow. To be happy.

I couldn't wait. So why with this new attitude was I contemplating reading Martin's personal thoughts? Did I really want to find out why my ex-husband started to hate me? See what he thought of me?

At times I thought there was a sadist in all of us that felt the need to understand why. Forget the hurt knowing would bring. I needed an answer. What did I do wrong?

I opened my dead husband's journal, invading

his privacy in a way I'd have never done when he lived, and became quickly confused. A few pages in and I realized this wasn't the story of a man who hated his life or his wife.

July thirteenth.

Work today was tough. Pretty sure the new boss hates me. But I can't let the family down. Geoff's birthday is coming up, and I am getting him that Power Wheel even if Omi doesn't think he needs it.

I paused for a moment, my throat tight. I'd forgotten about Omi. It was what Martin used to call me. Said Naomi was for strangers, but he was my best friend.

Tears pricked my eyes. Blubbering over the fact there was a time we were happy. When he loved me and the kids.

But something obviously changed.

I skimmed the next few months. Most of his posts were mundane and short summaries. Sometimes he'd skip days and write a longer paragraph. I even came across a random, *Love my wife. Love my life.*

Then the post for Geoff's birthday. Big boy turning two. And he got his Power Wheel.

His face was priceless. I knew Geoff would love the truck, and he is a natural behind the wheel. Omi screams every time he intentionally crashes into the bushes. Cracks

Geoff up each time. I love that kid. It would be nice to have another. Maybe a girl.

The statement hit me hard and made me wonder if I should get Winnie to read this. Her relationship with her dad had always been poor. Even as a baby, he never took to her like he did with Geoff. He tried, and yet at the same time, as the kids got older, he got meaner.

This small glimpse of a different Martin might help. The man might not have been good in his later years, but he didn't start out that way.

So what changed him?

I kept reading, summer rolling into the fall, and smiled at the picture he'd taped into the book. A Polaroid, because he hated waiting for film to get developed. This was a time before people documented everything with their phones. The comment under it. *My hot wife.*

It was me and Martin, dressed as Al and Peggy Bundy from *Married with Children*. It meant I had my hair teased and sprayed red. Hot pants and heels. Curvy, with my boobs shoved into some crazy cleavage. I looked healthy and, if padded, not yet fat. I'd lost most of my pregnancy weight from Geoff. Martin hugged me close and smiled wide. I recalled why.

A quickie in between taking little Geoff trick-ortreating around the block and before the sitter arrived to babysit our little guy, who was in bed. Martin hadn't been able to resist my ass, or so he claimed. We'd had a quick romp and then gone to an adult Halloween party. I'd said later on that was the night we conceived Winnie.

I flipped the page, and there was only a single line for November first.

Something happened last night. I think

The sentence didn't finish. Two weeks went by of nothing. A big gap given the previous half of the book. The next entry was November fifteenth, and it was a scrawling mess.

Why can't I remember? I know something happened. To me. To Omi. She's not been herself. And how does she not know where those bruises came from?

I froze, and my chest tightened. What was he talking about? What did he think happened at the Halloween block party? As far as I knew, we had fun. Hard to recall since I got wasted.

The next entry came three days later. *She's late.*

The words chilled me. Because that would have been when I suspected I was pregnant. A test confirmed it. We'd conceived Winnie.

The suspicion in my husband's mind fermented as my belly grew. He thought the baby wasn't his. That I'd cheated on him at that party.

Did I? I didn't remember much, but Martin kept living it over and over, his conjecture getting wild as it drove him slightly mad.

Does she not like having sex with me? Is that why she did what she did? Maybe nothing happened. Do I get a test done to see if it's mine?

At the time I hadn't seen his anxiety, or if I had, I ascribed it to stress. Martin had tried to keep it from me, but he spilled everything in his journal until March when he wrote:

I can't believe I forgot we had sex on Halloween. Omi reminded me when she asked if I wanted her to dress up as Peggy again. Maybe take me in the bathroom over the counter like I did on Halloween. She thinks that's the night we made the baby.

The next few months, he flipped back to happy Martin, and I was more confused than ever. The book ended with a picture of newborn Winnie with the caption, *Daddy's girl.*

My bath was still warm, yet I exited and did a naked run to my bedroom, leaving wet steps in my wake. I wanted the next book. What looked like a lot of reading didn't take much time with the looping large writing and pictures. It took only a second of sorting to find the next few years in the series.

Before I started reading, I added more hot

water to my bath. I planned to be a wrinkled prune by the time I got out.

The first book, I skimmed. Happy Martin. Happy. Happy. I found it when Winnie, around the age of five, had her tonsils removed.

She's the wrong blood type.

What did he mean?

It had been too long since I'd done biology. My phone came in handy for a search.

I read it over a few times, but the statement remained the same. I was O. Winnie was O. No idea about Geoff since he never had any major accidents. But I knew Martin was AB.

Shit.

Martin wasn't Winnie's dad.

6

I SLAMMED SHUT THE JOURNAL. NO WAY WAS Winnie reading this. Hell, I was fucking shaken. I'd just cemented my decision to set the damned lot of journals on fire and roast some Halloumi cheese over it since marshmallows weren't allowed on my diet.

Was Martin's behavior seriously because he thought I'd cheated on him and had someone else's child? That was insane. Why not confront me and deal with it head-on?

We could have done some genetic testing. Proven she belonged to us. I had no doubt she was mine. After all, I'd pushed her out, and as added proof, she looked a lot like I did at her age.

Martin, though, let his suspicion ferment rather than confront. Chose to hate us rather than leave.

Which made me think of things he'd said over the years. *"Too expensive to divorce you." "I ain't giving you half." "I'll kill you before I let you walk with a single red cent."*

In the end he'd tried to get rid of me and failed at it. It was pathetic and sad really that instead of being honest so we could work through it, he'd let jealousy turn him ugly.

If I wanted to take some of the blame, maybe instead of ignoring his obvious discontent, I should have tackled it head-on. I could have asked him what was wrong and pushed back when the verbal attitude and abuse started.

Could have. Should have.

The past was done. I lived in the now. And in the now, I wouldn't let anyone treat me like crap ever again.

The water in the tub sloshed as I shifted in agitation. My phone rang. I eyed it and leaned to see the screen.

Unknown number.

Don't answer. Probably a telemarketer. Who else would hide their identity?

I knew of one person who'd tried calling me three times since the store incident. He went to voicemail each time. Had he clued in I wasn't going to answer and hidden his identity?

The call ended. A moment later my phone vibrated.

I peeked. The symbol for a message appeared. And then a box with a text message, also from Unknown.

I didn't take you for a coward.

Had he met me? Biggest pussy around.

I frowned. I wasn't that person anymore.

You going to answer me, or are you too busy masturbating while picturing me between your legs.

My mouth rounded. *You're disgusting.* I couldn't help but reply.

Don't tell me you've never touched yourself.

Admit it? Never. *Go away, Kane.*

I knew you were thinking of me. How else would you know who this is?

I bit my lower lip before typing, *Only you ever disrespect me like this.*

Disrespect you by acknowledging you're an attractive woman?

I don't like it.

Liar.

How did he know his words gave me a cheap thrill? I was supposed to be strong. I didn't need a man. I didn't need validation. And yet, the fact he treated me as a desirable creature melted all kinds of inhibitions. I tingled between the legs. I wanted to touch myself, and it was his fault.

I furiously typed, *I told you to leave me alone.*

I can't.

Why? I paused before hitting Send. He wanted me to ask. Would probably reply with something filthy. And sexy.

I deleted my text and chose not to send a reply.

Naomi, my luscious witch, is your lack of reply because you're touching yourself in that big bathtub of yours?

How? I didn't realize I'd typed until I hit Send. I blinked.

How do I know where you are and what you're doing? Someone has to keep you safe. Watch over you so you can sleep.

Wait, did he imply… I rose from the tub, water sluicing from me, only to wonder if he had the right angle to see through the window. Never mind the lace curtains would confound, I dropped down hard enough to splash.

Did he skulk in my woods? And what did he mean keep me safe?

I don't need you spying on me.

Why spy when you'll invite me to share your bed soon enough.

Ha. Yup, I typed it, and I hoped it conveyed all

my disdain. In case it didn't, I added laughing emojis.

My phone lit up. *I'm going to screenshot this so that once we do become lovers you can apologize for being so stubborn and wrong. Let it be known, it can come in the form of oral or cookies. Homemade, preferably with chocolate chips.*

We will never be lovers.

I wager one day you'll be begging me to fuck you. To lick you head to toe and make you scream as you come for me.

It was utterly filthy, dirty, hot, and bothersome. I had two choices. Make myself come or confront the bastard harassing me. I threw on a sweatshirt and some leggings, my slick body making it hard to yank on, and stomped downstairs. I flung open the back door and yelled, "Where the hell are you?"

"Right here, waiting for my treat."

7

KANE SCARED THE PISS OUT OF ME ALMOST literally. I credit my masturbation of late for tightening that muscle enough I didn't end up with a flooding situation.

On the other hand, I almost died of a heart attack. My heart beat hard enough to almost come out of my chest.

I took my irritation out on him. "You!"

"Yes, me. Did you miss me?" he drawled, leaning on the post holding up my porch roof.

"Like you miss a wart once you've frozen it off."

He didn't seem perturbed. He grinned, a wide smile in that craggy face. "Still protesting too much. Admit it. You want me."

"I came outside to tell you to fuck off."

"Now, sweetheart."

I waved my hand. "Don't you start with that sweetheart shit. My name is Naomi, or better yet, Ms. Rousseaux."

"I'd say we're too intimate for that."

"We're nothing. But you're a pest. This is harassment."

He laughed. "So have me charged."

"I have a better idea." Make that hex or two I might try. "How attached are you to your hair?"

He grabbed his chest. "And here all I'm trying to do is protect you."

I snorted. "Sexual harassment hardly keeps me safe."

"It's only harassment if you're not enjoying it."

I gaped at him. "That is the most misogynistic thing I've ever heard."

"And you're cute when you're pretending to be offended."

"I am not pretending!" I huffed hotly. Part lie. I did get too much of a thrill from his ardent pursuit. I needed to work on my self-esteem obviously.

"If you say so, sweetheart."

"Stop calling me that!" I wouldn't admit it was cute. It should have been Darryl saying it, not Kane.

"Ask me nicely."

I glared.

He laughed.

"You still haven't said why you're really here."

"Protection."

"Against?"

"Forces of darkness."

"I thought you took care of them the other night." It occurred to me that with him on my doorstep, I could quickly ask a few questions then send him on his way. While he kept disarming me with words, he kept far enough away that I wasn't overwhelmed by his presence.

"While we did make a dent, it wasn't enough to permanently rout them. They were thwarted but will try again."

"And who is this 'they'?"

He pressed his lips into a line. "Best you don't know. Already there are too many involved."

"You're not making any sense."

"Because it's too complicated to explain."

"Then what can you tell me?" I asked with exasperation.

"You're in danger."

"From what? Because my biggest threat is dead."

He snorted. "Your ex-husband was hardly the worthy villain."

"Says a huge villain."

"That would depend on perception. Some would call me hero."

My turn to make a sound. "I can't see that happening; you're too bad."

"I know." He smirked.

"Does this have to do with The Chill?"

"The what?"

"The Chill? When the world around me goes frosty and it feels like some big, crushing presence is trying to squash me."

The corners of his eyes crinkled. "An apt name for an ancient construct."

"You know what it is."

"It's not the thing you should fear the most."

"And what would that be?"

"I really shouldn't say." He played coy. I wanted to smack him, but that would require getting close.

"How do you know these things? What do you know about magic?"

"Ditch Darryl and I'll teach you." He purred the words, and I shivered. I had a feeling his kind of magic didn't involve clothes.

"I am not dumping Darryl."

"Your loss. Now if you don't mind, you're very distracting and I should be paying attention."

I dared any woman to not preen under that praise. "No one's making you stay."

"Exactly. I'm here protecting you despite the fact you're determined to hate me."

"I don't hate you." Not anymore. My feelings were much too complex for that.

His expression sobered. "I wish I could tell you more, but there is a reason your grandmother never told you about your heritage. A reason why she let you leave."

"Is this where you tell me I should have never come back?"

He shook his head. "You can't hide from fate."

Was he alluding to us again? He and I weren't fated to be anything but adversaries.

"I'm going inside. Alone. You should go home, too."

"Who says I ever left?" He offered an enigmatic smile. "Sweet dreams, sweetheart, may they be about me."

"Never."

"When you touch yourself, imagine it is my fingers. Yell my name when you come."

"You are unbelievable." I stepped away from him. "Good night, Kane."

"Yes, good night. Brother."

The scythe came out nowhere.

8

I SCREAMED BEFORE I REALIZED KANE REMAINED intact, more or less. The oversized blade went right through him. He dissipated as if comprised of mist.

A ghost? Shit, had he died?

I didn't know I said it aloud until Jace replied, "No, not dead. A mirage that won't happen again if you add the right protection to the property."

I gaped at Jace, who stood there with a reaper-like scythe. I couldn't help it. "What the fuck is wrong with you? You tried to kill your brother."

"Not even close. As you noticed, he's not here."

Good to know I'd not imagined Kane. Bad to know I never even guessed I'd not been dealing with the real thing. It meant my attraction to him wasn't just some kind of in-person pheromone thing. He had the ability to set me off balance.

That didn't mean I welcomed Jace's intrusion. "What are you doing, swinging a knife around?"

"Scythe."

"Sharp freaking object. What if you'd sliced me?"

"It would have hurt."

I stared at him before finally saying, "Are you for real?"

"Very, unlike Kane just now. I don't know what he was thinking."

"He said he was protecting me."

Jace snorted. "The only person Kane cares about is himself."

"He's your brother."

"Half."

Like Winnie and Geoff. Would it change their relationship if they knew?

"How did Kane do that?" A hologram projection was my first thought, but that would involve some heavy tech.

Jace appeared as if he wouldn't answer at first, and then he sighed. "You know how he did it."

"Magic," I said hesitantly as if the word spoken aloud might bite me.

Jace didn't mock me. "Mostly. Astral walking is an ability only some can tap."

"Astral walking, that's when a soul leaves a body to go exploring."

"More or less."

"Can you do it?"

"No." Jace didn't elaborate.

"You know about magic," I persisted. Maybe I didn't need Kane for answers. I could ask the next best thing.

"I do."

It was like pulling teeth with shitty dental floss that kept breaking. "Care to elaborate?"

"No."

"You're hardly being helpful," I grumbled. "You don't talk to me in days, almost kill me, and then it's like riddle me this. As if you're part sphinx."

"The sphinxes weren't that clever."

"Holy crap, did you just make a joke?" I exaggerated by grabbing my chest in shock and pretending to fall over.

"Doubtful. I find very little amusing."

"Aren't you just a ray of sunshine." And to think this dour man had been a guy I'd been eyeballing when I first moved in. He'd been shoved aside in favor of Daryl. Heck, even Kane had more personality. At least Kane wasn't always trying to get me to leave Cambden, more like getting me to drop my pants.

"I don't know what you expect of me. You keep acting as if everything is fine. And perfect."

"Are you here to tell me it's not?" was my sarcastic retort.

"No point since it falls on deaf ears. You made your choice to stay, and now the consequence is yours to bear."

"Implying I made the wrong one and now I'll die?"

"Death would have been kinder than what some have planned."

The starkness of his statement demanded explanation, but before I could ask, Geoff emerged, dressed in a track suit and wearing a concerned expression. "Mom, everything okay? Is this guy bugging you?"

"You know Jace." I jerked a thumb in his direction.

"Yeah, I do, but if he's bothering you…" My son slewed a dark glance at my neighbor. Coming to his mother's rescue. Sweet but not necessary. Not to mention, it wasn't as if my son could do much to the scythe-wielding Jace.

I shook my head. "I'm fine. Jace was just leaving. He came by because he thought he heard something."

"And chose to go Grim Reaper instead of grabbing a gun?" Geoff said.

"I don't use firearms." Jace used more than a few syllables. Mark it on a calendar.

"You should see him with an axe," I joked.

Neither man seemed impressed with my humorous abilities.

My son took on a caveman role. "Mom, why don't you go inside while I see Jace home."

"Pretty sure Jace knows the way."

Again, I got a dual-testosterone stare. I shrugged. "Whatever."

I headed inside but didn't go far, watching from the door as Geoff and Jace headed off. They stopped by the woods separating the properties and argued. My son's hands waved. Jace remained still, arms crossed, gripping his ridiculous scythe. Add in a cloak and he was ready for Halloween.

Pride filled me that my son had such a chivalrous streak. Brave, too, confronting Jace. I could only hope my neighbor wouldn't snap and kill my son.

Instead, Jace held out the oversized knife, and Geoff took it then kept watch as Jace crossed back to his property. Only then did my son glance at the house. I doubted he could see me. He used the scythe as a staff as he returned. Before he could catch me spying, I fled up the stairs to my room, wondering what Jace had said to Geoff that convinced my son to accept the scythe.

In my room, I found one last text message from Kane.

Sweet dreams.

More like wet ones.

9

I awoke in a puddle. I couldn't have said what that puddle was comprised of. Could be cum, given I throbbed between my legs. I'd not been this horny since I got boobs.

Funny how the more I climaxed, the more I craved it. I began to see why some people did it so often. How had I forgotten the relief that came with a good orgasm?

I brought my little purple bullet into the shower but tossed it aside in favor of the showerhead. Put that thing on massage and I was riding it like a cowgirl, trying not to yell yeehaw.

My climax hit me hard, and I leaned into the tile wall, breathing hard, picturing Darryl, but having to concentrate because Kane kept trying to interfere.

Damn him.

Exiting the bathroom, with my hair pulled in a messy wet bun, I found a text on my phone from Winnie saying she was staying at her new friend's place and would pop by during the day to grab some clothes. Didn't sound as if I'd see her.

It seemed so fast. Was this how things worked? I didn't think I'd be comfortable sleeping over at the house of someone I'd just met.

It made me glad Darryl didn't mind taking things slow. Maybe a touch too slow. The opposite of Kane, who kept pushing. What was his angle? I didn't believe for a moment Kane's claim of being consumed by desire for me. He wanted something.

If it weren't for Darryl, I might have dared him to show off his supposed prowess.

Good thing I had Darryl. Now if only I could enjoy more of him. A shudder went through me as if I'd not just come less than twenty minutes ago.

Dammit. These days I wore panty liners, so I didn't juice the fabric. My lube jar would dry up at this rate.

Heading downstairs, I found a note from Geoff saying he'd gamed late and would be sleeping in. Only my cat was on hand to greet me, twining around my ankles, eager for his breakfast.

I crouched and made him wait so I could pet

him. The soft stroke of his fur was a pleasure. When I opened the cupboard, he started to purr.

"Listen to you," I chided. "Your love affair with food is getting a little out of hand."

I would know. I'd relied on it a little too much rather than dealing with my emotions.

My travel mug didn't take long to fill, and soon I was headed into the shop. I might be playing hooky that afternoon, but I could salvage part of the day.

Passing the gas station, I didn't see Darryl's truck. Not in. Again.

Odd, because for months before that he'd always been there every day before eight, without fail. Was something making him sleep in? Someone that wasn't me?

My hands tightened on the wheel, and I heard a high-pitched hum in my ears. My jealousy roiled inside me, and for a second, I thought of Martin. Was this how he'd felt? Betrayed. And for what?

No proof.

I was getting upset simply because Darryl wasn't parked at his work. Shades of psycho stalker. I needed to cool it. Hadn't the man been by to see me just the day before to steal a kiss?

Leaving the gas station behind in my rearview, it wasn't long until I saw smoke threading into the sky. I pulled over as the wail of a siren screamed from behind. I remained on the side of the road, clutching the wheel, dread pitting in my stomach. Eventually, as the smoke lessened, I pulled back onto Main Street.

The trucks and gawkers were blocking the road. The hum inside me threatened to make me explode because I knew whose store got hit by fire.

Always with the fucking fire. But this time, it really stung. That shop had been one hundred percent me. My do-over. My chance to prove my worth.

Ashes.

The fire truck idled out front, and people milled, pushing against a caution line to watch. I parked and jumped out, running to get as close as I could. When the cop would have stopped me, I exclaimed, "That's my shop."

"Sorry, ma'am."

Sorry? That store was my baby. My second chance. Gone.

So unfair.

It took a moment to register that someone was speaking to me. "What?" I turned a dazed and confused look on Officer Murphy, who bore an impressive mustache and partial beard, a rugged and wide man, and I'd never much entertained thoughts of sleeping with him, mostly because our encounters always involved trouble.

"I said"—his voice lifted to cut through the din around us—"most of the damage is smoke related."

"Meaning everything is ruined." I rubbed my forehead, massaging the tight spot. "It will take months to fix. A good chunk of the stock will have to be tossed out." Things like furniture might clean up, but books and other more delicate items would be ruined.

"At first glance, it seems like the fire started in the back, by your electrical panel."

"Guess I should contact my insurance company." Did my policy cover electrical fire? I'd soon find out.

Officer Murphy wasn't done with me. "Where were you around seven this morning?"

"Why?"

"Just answer the question, ma'am."

Did he seriously ma'am me? I stared at Officer Murphy and his gruff mien. "Don't tell me you think I set this fire."

"We have to look at all possibilities."

"You just said it started by the electrical box."

"Never said it was a malfunction, though."

"You think it's arson. Probably the same person

who kept messing with my sign." They'd done it enough times I worried they'd strike again.

"You can't assume they're related." My cautious policeman, who'd yet to catch anyone. That might be part of the reason why I didn't want to climb him like a tree. Murphy just kept disappointing me.

"You don't think it's odd that it's always my shop being targeted?"

"Coincidence at best."

"How many times before it's a pattern?" I flung my hands.

"Could be someone getting back at you because of the curse," he opined.

"Do not refer to that stupid curse." I thought I was done dealing with the small-town gossip mill that claimed my family was descended of witches. Times like these, I wished I could cast a spell and make everything all right.

Officer Murphy was called away, leaving me to stand alone in a crowd. Literally, people Many glanced in my direction, but none would meet my gaze or talk to me. I would have sworn I heard a whispered "witch."

Great. How many people thought I'd done this? Never mind it made no sense. Why would I burn my store?

I trudged back to my car, the old urge to

collapse and cry strong. For a moment, I thought of getting a bottle of booze and drinking it until I fell over. In the movies, heroes did it all the time. Got drunk to deal with the trauma of life. But then I'd have a hangover to contend with, maybe some puke and whatever questionable decisions I made. What if I slept with the wrong guy?

Last time I got that wasted, my husband was convinced I'd cheated on him.

Would I cheat on Darryl?

I should hope not. But that wasn't the reason I chose not to get blasted out of my mind. Drinking wouldn't fix anything. Only I could.

Once I reached my house, I dug out the insurance policy and began making calls. Fuck whoever set my shop on fire. I wouldn't give up. Not now. Not ever.

Talking to the adjuster proved less painful than expected. Geoff appeared to still be sleeping. Winnie was at her new friend's, and Grisou chose a patch of sunlight over me.

A shower removed the smell of smoke that I couldn't seem to shake. I moved about in autonomous mode, ignoring texts from Trish. I read but didn't reply to Darryl's, *Sorry about the shop. See you later.*

Why not now? Wasn't I more important?

The only one who didn't send me a message was Kane.

It disappointed me more than it should have.

I barely tasted my lunch, which consisted of some avocado oil, pan-fried broccoli, seasoned and served with a melted cheese sauce, minced jalapeno, a dollop of sour cream, and sprinkles of bacon. Usually one of my favorite lunches. My spirit and appetite just weren't into it.

I found myself walking down to the lake, having to forge a path in the light snow, my boots crunching the surface and sinking into the soft ground inches below. The air hung still and frozen. Not harsh enough to hurt the lungs when breathed, but I puffed mist.

Winter truly gripped the land. The lake wore a solid surface of ice. The snow cover on it was seamless, lacking even animal tracks. The mill wouldn't be mining for anything during the winter. Which reminded me, their product was set to launch soon. Bottled mud. Something with medicinal purposes, not that I knew how it worked. I'd played around with the mud from the lake, made pottery with it that I fired in a kiln. Worked it with my hands. Never fixed anything with me. Not my sagging boobs or flubbery belly. The paper cut on my hand didn't miraculously heal.

So what exactly did the mud do? I'd never really looked into it. Surely there'd be a review for it somewhere on the internet. Maybe my mud wasn't as good as the stuff they'd been excavating at the deepest part of the lake.

I should get my hands on a bottle. Kane would probably give me one if I asked.

I wouldn't ask.

Huff. My puff of breath hung in front of me, a reminder of the cold that told me I should have worn a hat and gloves. I pulled up my hood and shoved my hands into my pockets.

Of all the places to live, I'd chosen a cold one. Not somewhere tropical or even temperate all year round. However, I doubted anywhere else would have rivaled Cambden. There was something alive about this place. As if the location resonated with my soul. It whispered to me.

As I stared across the icy expanse, I saw swirls of movement. Nothing was there, but there was chatter. Hushed sounds. As if the place tried to speak to me.

I knelt and placed my hand on the crusting snow. Cold. Blank. Nothing jumped out at me.

But the restless feeling wouldn't leave. I needed an outlet. A spell.

I leaned forward and traced a sigil I'd seen in

the recipe book before I lost it. The name of the concoction that shared the page with the mark was Total Recall. Which made me giggle as I thought of Arnie in that movie set on Mars.

Curious, I'd tried making the soup following the recipe on that page. Ate a big bowl of the savory stuff, I didn't get flooded with recollections, but the shape on the recipe page stuck with me.

Could it help me remember? I wanted to know everything. I traced it. Round and round, loop left and over, then again to deepen the lines because a strong spell demanded perfection. By the time I was done I'd recreated a fair impression.

Total recall time. I leaned forward and touched my tongue to the starting point, saliva to charge it. I blew hotly to activate it.

Nothing happened. I spat on the mark, making sure it didn't mess up any lines. Nothing. What would it take to fire it up? Blood?

I eyed my paper cut. Gotten the day before and barely scabbed over. Would I really gash myself for a spell that didn't work?

The red smear answered that question. I kept the open wound pressed to the mark and spoke aloud, "Show me what I can't remember. Show me everything."

The mark ignited in blue flames that startled,

but I couldn't pull free. My hand was stuck. The flames licked higher, and in their dancing tendrils, I could see…

Me and my dad on this beach, picking rocks. Nice flat ones that would skip across the surface.

A younger me, holding Grandma's hand as we kick at the water.

A woman bolting from the woods, a bundle in her arms, racing to the water's edge and flinging her package.

A baby.

It was me. I hit the surface with a splash.

A moment later, Grandma was in the water, swimming for me. My mother was on the shore, screaming and tearing at her hair until my dad arrived and pinned her arms to her side.

It wasn't the only time she tried to drown me. *The next time I was a few years old and she held me under water, sobbing, "I'm sorry."*

I was done with the past. I didn't want to see, but the magic wouldn't let go. My back arched as more memories slammed into me.

I was shown two generations before mine, when Grandma was a girl, playing on the beach. Then her mother. But that's not all I was shown. When my family line was done, time rewound, and I was shown the lake through the ages.

The glow on it appeared in sporadic bursts, spewing forth the monster, a real living creature, not a machine.

Maddy chained and made captive. I sob as they whip her, cry as she bugles her torment. The proud beast turns into obedient captive, working for her tormentors until she died on the beach.

Then time rewound again.

Before her capture. I went backwards to a time when Maddy swam free, but only for a short while in each generation. Maddy would rise, feed, then slumber again, a hidden guardian to whatever hid in the bottom of the lake.

Time continued to scroll, but I could no longer process the small details, not when bombarded by every single season with their freezes and thaws. The hundreds, then thousands of sunrises and sunsets. My mind filled. Expanded. And still more memories unspooled, covering the ones I had, wiping and writing over, then wiping and—

Snap. The sudden severance of the spell had me gasping and blinking, before I fell face first into the snow.

10

I woke in my bed, the ceiling above familiar, the voice by my side unexpected but welcome.

"About time you woke. I was getting worried."

"Darryl?" I tilted my head and almost moaned at the pain roiling through it. My stomach heaved, and I really hoped I wasn't about to barf in Darryl's lap. It could be a relationship breaker.

He clasped my hand and leaned over me, all concern. "Of course, it's me. I came as soon as Trish called me for help."

"Trish?" I frowned. "What happened?"

"You tell me. When you weren't answering your phone, she came by to find you. Said you were by the lake, passed out in the snow."

"I—" I didn't actually remember what

happened. Last I recalled I'd been going for a walk to clear my mind. "How did she find me?"

"She didn't. Apparently, when she opened the door, your cat lost its shit and ran out."

Of course, Trish bolted after Grisou, who knew his owner was injured and led her to me. I'd have to feed him extra special treats.

"What were you doing by the lake?" he asked sharply.

I blinked. Why did he sound mad? Then it hit me. Because he cared. "I wasn't doing anything." I had a sudden flash of Arnie the actor. He had that movie he did that I loved. Total…

I paused as I recalled trying to cast a spell. Had I overdone it with my magic? Judging by the throb in my head, I had magic hangover.

But it did have one positive. Look who hovered over me.

Darryl gripped my hand. "You have to stay away from the lake. It's not safe there for you."

"It's not safe anywhere apparently, or did you forget my shop got torched?"

"Maybe it's a sign you should take a break. Stay home, inside."

Once upon a time, I did that. I shoved myself up in bed. "I am not hiding away. I'll fix it and be back in business in no time. That's what insurance is for."

"Will it pay fair market value for *my* things?" he emphasized. "My understanding is all the goods are ruined."

"I've yet to conduct a full assessment, and the insurance will send their people in, too. But don't worry, you'll get your fair share." Was he really going to complain about money at a time like this?

"I didn't mean to complain," he hastened to assure me. "The important thing is no one was hurt."

I disagreed on the hurt part. I'd felt the blow. "The cops are checking to see if someone set the fire."

"Arson?" he scoffed. "More likely your kiln." An old pizza oven I'd been using to fire my newfound pottery habit.

"Whereas I'm hoping faulty wiring." Because I was pretty sure my insurance would cover it.

"It could have been any number of things," he agreed. "But you're safe, if banned from going on walks alone."

"I'm fine."

"Let's make sure of that." He patted my hand in a way that was more father than lover. Ugh. He glanced at the stairs. "Would you like me to fetch someone so you're not alone when I leave?"

"I thought Trish was here."

"She was, but she left to handle something."

"Then maybe you should stay a while longer." I clutched at his hand because it occurred to me that I had Darryl in my bedroom. Me and him and a bed. I also had a pasty mouth and probably bedhead.

"Stay…" He glanced away then back. "Of course."

Oh, shit he said yes. "Can you give me a second. I need a drink." Before he could offer to fetch me something, I rolled out of bed and noticed the knees of my pants were soaked and cold, a reminder I'd been kneeling in snow. I'd only been stripped out of my coat and boots. I closed the door to the bathroom and wished I had access to fresh clothes. I brushed my teeth and gargled quickly. By the time I turned around to dry my face and hands, there was a pair of pants hanging on the bar with the towel.

Thank you, house!

The leggings were warm, as if from the dryer, and kept parts of me tucked in the right places. When I emerged, it was to see Darryl sitting on the window seat, rooting through Martin's old box, which I'd have sworn I hadn't left lying out.

"What are you doing?"

He lifted his head only briefly. "You keep your ex-husband's stuff in your room." Stated, not even a query.

It roused an irritation in me. "You shouldn't be looking through my things."

"Why not? Is it because you're hiding something from me?"

Did he really accuse me? "I have nothing to hide."

"Don't you?" He swept his hand at the box. "Are you pining over your failed marriage?"

The term failed hit me hard. "I didn't screw it up." How dare he even say so?

As if Darryl realized he'd gone too far, his face turned apologetic. "I'm sure you didn't. I shouldn't have let my jealousy speak for me," he soothed.

My bruised ego soaked up the praise, but at the same time, I remained annoyed. I'd never seen this side to Darryl before. "Martin and I grew apart."

"It happens. His loss, my gain." Offered with a smile. "Obviously, there was something wrong with the man to not realize what kind of gem you are."

"You think I'm a gem?"

"Precious and rare," he stated, grabbing my

hands. He drew me to him, sitting me on his lap, which thrilled me to no end.

"Thanks for coming to my rescue and carrying me." I cupped his face and smiled.

"You're welcome." The proper respectful thing to say, and yet for some reason, I could hear a mocking Kane saying, *Thank me with your tongue.*

Maybe I would. Before I could chicken out, I kissed Darryl. He kissed me back, and excited, I groaned against his lips, squirmed against him. Maybe he'd get the hint.

Instead of taking off my clothes, he pulled away. "We can't."

"What's wrong?" I asked.

"You should be resting."

"I'm fine," I protested.

"You've suffered an ordeal," he insisted, stroking my hair back. "Give yourself time to recover."

"Kissing you helps me relax." I was bold.

He laughed softly. "But the things kissing make me want to do are anything but. I'll wait until you're one hundred percent."

He was such a gentleman. He put me back to bed and kissed me on the forehead saying he'd see me tomorrow.

I heard the front door close then his truck as he

left. I couldn't sleep. What happened by the water? Had I cast a spell that knocked me out?

I wandered out of my bed, restless and not tired despite what Darryl seemed to think. I sat in the window seat and noticed the pile of journals. I grabbed one written in the last few years.

February 14th. I told her I had to work, and she believed it. As if I'd want to be with her when I could have my Helena.

I frowned. How odd that Martin's girlfriend had the same name as Geoff's. Surely a weird coincidence.

I skipped ahead.

June. I am so ready to leave her, but Helena talked me out of it. Said it's not the right time yet. Soon. At least the whore's brat is gone.

I winced and tossed the journal to the floor. I leaned my head against the window, gazing outside.

There was movement in the trees, and I held my breath until the form emerged, dressed all in black so that only the paler countenance of his face appeared. Kane saluted me with a sword.

Back to guard me.

Funny how the thought helped me go to sleep.

11

THE NEXT MORNING, I CAME DOWNSTAIRS TO FIND Geoff in the kitchen putting breakfast on the table. Scrambled eggs with cheese, bacon, fried tomato slices, and even some sausage.

"Oh, that looks amazing!" I declared. "You didn't have to make me food, though."

"Yeah I did. I didn't even know you suffered a seizure by the water until Winnie told me."

"You saw Winnie?"

"Yeah, she popped in early this morning to grab some things."

"She's gone again?" It shouldn't have surprised me, but... Okay, yeah, it did. I would have thought she'd have stuck around to at least check on me.

"Don't change the subject. Are you okay? Why didn't anyone come tell me downstairs?"

"I'm sure Trish just forgot."

As had Darryl. Which made me wonder why Trish would think to call Darryl before my son. I thought those two had a close relationship. Trish certainly implied it with all the details she knew of his life.

"Forgot, my ass. She's still pissed at me."

"Why?" I exclaimed. This was the first I'd heard of it.

"Because of something that happened with Helena."

There was my opening. "What happened?"

"A few things." He slid into the spot across from me, suddenly nervous.

"What's wrong?" I tried to keep it short and simple. Didn't want to scare him off with my eagerness to mother him.

"I wasn't entirely truthful about why I'm here. I mean I did want to see you for Christmas, but the real reason I came is because I lost my job."

"I'm sorry, Geoff, what happened?" Because my understanding was that he worked for some hip new startup that was going places.

"Mismanagement of the company led to them going into bankruptcy. I lost my last two paychecks as a result. With it being Christmas, no one was hiring, and since I didn't have enough for January rent, I abandoned my apartment."

My nosy ass couldn't resist the opening. "What about your fiancée, Helena?"

"We are on a break."

For a second, I flashed back to Ross on *Friends*. "That's got to be hard." A subtle nudge to see if he'd explain. Especially since he'd taken a call from her a few nights ago.

"I know you're wondering why. I mean, on her birthday, I asked her to marry me. We were planning to get hitched in May. It's just…" He raked his fingers through his hair. "I discovered things about her. Weird stuff that's made me rethink things."

"Like?" Did she lick the flavor off chips and put them back in the bag? I'd read about it in a Dear Somebody column. It was a deal breaker for some.

"She thinks she's a witch."

I almost choked but turned it into a cough. "A witch?" I gasped. "Oh, how, um, different." Now was probably not the time to tell him he was descended from a long line of them, according to the book in my bedroom. Nor was I about to admit that the stupid genealogy book had his sister's daddy listed as someone that wasn't Martin. I'd never cheated on my husband. Ever.

"It's more than different. She believes it. Thinks she does magic. Wants me to do stuff with her."

"Have you?" I asked. What did my son know? Had he exhibited powers?

"'Course not. It's bullshit," he exclaimed, only to add, "Sorry. I don't mean to swear, but seriously, magic? It doesn't exist." Geoff sounded just like me. Would he prove to be as stubborn?

"What if I said magic is real?" I ventured cautiously.

"I'd say your eyes are brown because you're full of poop."

My lips twitched. "They're brown because of genetics, and FYI, since you hadn't heard, you're descended from a long line of witches. Or warlocks. I don't know what the proper terminology is in our family."

"How about crazy? Since when do you think you ride a broom?"

"One, no stick is getting wedged by my cheeks, and two, I found out about my family's reputation only when I returned. Apparently, we're some kind of lake guardians." And I'd failed. Maddy the monster had died.

"We're pagan environmentalists?" he joked, but I'd seen too much to deny it.

"Our family is special. We have abilities."

"Mom, do you need to talk to someone?" Geoff took my hand and softened his tone.

I yanked my hand free. "What? No, of course not."

"Do I have to worry about you sacrificing animals or dancing naked and scaring the neighbors?"

"Don't be silly." I'd definitely never dance naked.

"Do you think you can fly?"

"You know I'm afraid of heights."

"Helena isn't. She told me she can fly. And cast spells. Says if I join her, I can be part of the new world. That when magic returns, I can join the ranks of royalty."

"Oh." I could see where he questioned his fiancée's sanity. Old me would have totally agreed. New me understood there were things that seemed impossible but were true. Perhaps his fiancée really was a practicing witch. Kind of wished I'd met her now. Could she help me with some of my questions?

Geoff kept talking. "Anyhow, I told Helena I needed a break and came to see you. I was hoping I could hang until I find a job and a place."

"You can stay as long as you need." The house

would accommodate, and I got to reconnect with my son.

Win. Win.

And then just because I couldn't help myself, "Did you know your dad had a girlfriend?"

And just like that I lost the mom of the year award.

Geoff froze, stepped away from me. "I didn't talk much to Dad."

"I wasn't sure. I mean…" I blustered ahead. "We didn't talk much either. So I didn't know what was going on." Then because my foot just needed to be shoved in my mouth, "Her name was Helena."

Geoff stared at me. "It's a common name, Mom."

It was, and yet it nagged at me, especially since I had no way of checking it out to reassure myself. Martin hated social media, so I'd never seen a picture of his girlfriend.

"Weird coincidence, huh?" I tried to laugh it off.

He didn't look amused.

Great. Maybe I should make him some brownies. Later. I had stuff to do.

With it being the thirtieth, I had only one more day before New Year's with Darryl. I couldn't wait. How sweet that he'd come to see me when he thought me injured. And so solicitous of me. Never taking advantage.

The jerk.

Would it kill him to seduce me? I swear if he didn't do something soon, I'd get a complex.

Surely, he wasn't stalling on purpose. I might not have dated in a long time, but I had faith I read his intentions properly. He desired me. He was just waiting for the right time.

The right time better be tomorrow. Which reminded me. I hadn't gone shopping for underwear or a dress. Crap. I wondered if I could still talk Trish into going.

However, I also had to get inside my store and begin the onerous task of cleaning it out and planning repairs. The other option was to sulk around my house and eyeball the food I couldn't have.

The urge welled within me to stuff my face for the high and lull that came with eating carbs. The pleasure of the sugar. Real stuff, not the fake that took getting used to. The crunch of a French fry. Nothing on the low carb diet could replace it. Bread. Fluffy, fresh from the oven, buttered, bread.

So good, I'd put on over a hundred and twenty some pounds. Felt trapped in my body. Being overweight was a catch twenty-two. It wasn't just getting your mind to cooperate. You needed the body to work. The extra person I was carting around really dragged me down. It wasn't that I lacked strength, more that it was buried in weight.

It hurt my joints. My limbs. In my forties, I huffed and strained to do things that other people did with ease.

Don't eat.

I wouldn't go back to that life. Yes, I was stressed. I could handle it. What was the worst that could happen?

I might lose the store and have to get a job. That would suck. But I'd survive.

What was the best-case scenario?

The shop wouldn't take as much as I feared to fix.

And I could control part of that by heading there this morning to assess the damage and start working. Maybe I'd visit my witch forum and see if there was a spell to clean up the mess. What bummed me out was delaying my day out with the girls. I'd been looking forward to it, but as a business woman, I had to set my priorities.

I went under the kitchen sink to find a cleaning bucket, some rags, garbage bags, and general-purpose cleaner. There was also an engraving tool, the version that plugged into a wall and heated a nail-like head. It could burn wood. In this case, flooring to set sigils.

Thank you. So cool. The house provided before I even knew what I needed.

As I walked past the door to Winnie's room, I noticed it slightly ajar. Geoff said she'd been by to grab some stuff.

A peek inside the crack showed the bed, neatly made, her clothes folded on a chair sitting beside it. Beside the door was a wastepaper basket filled with crumpled paper. She'd been working on something. I grabbed the handle of the door to close it, only to notice a word written on a discarded ball of paper garbage.

Fire. The loopy scrawl was Wendy's. I reached for it and smoothed out the sheet. Beside the word fire was a symbol I recognized. It was part of the one I'd recently drawn for light.

It made sense, light and heat being related. Under fire, another sigil labelled, "Wind." A comment beside said, "Can propel or repel. Located on the roof, used by the tiles to prevent damage?"

Wait a second. Winnie had studied the sigils in the house? She never told me. Then again, why would she? I had more or less mocked the spells she'd tried to replicate from the recipe book. She didn't understand my epiphany. That not only did I now believe but I also wielded magic.

Should I tell her the things I'd experienced and seen? Would she believe me?

I knew Kane would.

Bending, I retrieved more balled sheets from the basket. Winnie had drawn symbols I'd seen around the house, and some I hadn't. She hypothesized their meaning, crossing things out as she dug deeper. A few she slashed and scrawled, "Fuck this." I assumed it meant she couldn't decipher it.

How had I not known she was doing this? Had she tried to activate any of the sigils? Did she have the same magic I did?

And for a moment, the horrible person in me was jealous that perhaps I wasn't special. That my child would take it away.

The wrongness of it filled me with guilt. Why shouldn't my daughter achieve great things? We could share this. The Rousseaux witches, doing magic together.

It made me want to seek her out and tell her everything. Explain our roots. Maybe omit the father part. We'd cry and hug. Make high protein waffles together.

I kept her drawings as I rose from the bed where I'd unconsciously sat. I took a step to the door and saw it. Opened wide on the desk. Grandma's missing book of spells. It never even occurred to me Winnie would have taken it. Why hadn't she said anything when I'd mentioned it being lost?

As I entered her room, and neared the book, was when I noticed the damage, the sliced edges of sheets where pages had been removed. A utility knife sat beside it, a damning clue as to the culprit.

Why had Winnie done this? It boggled the mind. One did not just cut stuff out of a family heirloom. Maybe I'd not instilled her with a sacred duty toward the written word, but surely, she knew how wrong it was to desecrate a book like this.

I grabbed the tome and flipped through it, searching for more damaged spots. Only the single section. Four pages in total. No idea what used to be on them.

I tucked the book to my chest. How would I deal with this?

It wasn't Winnie taking it that bothered me. I would have loaned it if she asked. But to destroy it was wrong on so many levels.

It also raised another point. If Winnie had gone into my room and taken the spell book, she might have glanced through the family tree.

I doubted she could have read it. After all it,

took a combination of a ring that I wore on a chain around my neck and UV light to see anything.

What about Martin's books though? I glanced at the ceiling. I should hide those in a better place. The family tree and Martin's musings went into the trunk of my car. I'd leave them there until I could properly dispose of them.

I drove into town and parked by my shop. Standing outside the front door, I took a deep breath. Time to see the damage.

It turned out better than expected. Especially where I'd drawn my circle of protection. It remained untouched and appeared to mitigate the issue even a few feet out from it. The back was a sooty write-off, but luckily, I kept the antiques wrapped. Fingers crossed it was enough to seal them off from damage.

I could fix this with a little bit of elbow work.

I set my bucket down, rolled up my sleeves, and started searching for cleaning companies. I had some funds left over from the divorce, and if my insurance paid like it should, I'd be reimbursed. Especially if I kept the claims reasonable. The place didn't need a gutting but a good mop and wipe.

I also added more spells.

1 2

As I used the wood-burning tool to engrave the very edges of my store, I couldn't help but notice the number of people pausing outside my shop, trying the door despite the closed sign. It killed me. I so wanted to be able to greet them and match them with something they just had to have.

I didn't think I'd be out of business for too long. Most of the damage was soot related. The cleaning company said they'd have it done by January third: walls, shelves, counters, and the salvageable items. The painters could come in the fourth, giving me a few days to find some new stock.

Ironically enough, my sign survived intact.

Darryl came to see me mid-morning, knocking on the door until I glanced over and saw him smiling in my direction. Butterflies exploded in my tummy.

I set down my cleaning rag and let him in. "Darryl. I wasn't expecting you." I probably looked a mess.

"Thought I'd check in, especially given your incident last night. I'm surprised you're here today."

My shoulders lifted and dropped. "Better I get started than mope at home."

"You work too hard."

"I like it, though." I really did. A sense of purpose really helped.

"So the reason I popped in was because of something strange. Remember that puzzle box I gave you to sell?" Darryl queried.

Of course I remembered it. Stupid thing disappeared on me the night the imps attacked my house. I'd been thinking of telling him I'd sold it and paying for it out of my own pocket. Should I lie? Did he know?

I blinked as he pulled the missing puzzle box out of his pocket. "If I didn't know better, I'd say this is mine."

"Where did you find it?" I blurted out, grabbing for it, only to grimace. It vibrated in my grip, the sensation unpleasant.

"Well, that's the weird part. In my truck after I got home from your place last night."

Had my house placed it there? "Thank goodness you found it. I wondered where it had gone. Darned Grisou. He's worse than a magpie, stealing stuff and hiding it." I lied my face off rather than tell him I'd lost it and my magical house gave it back.

"Why was it at your house? Shouldn't it be in the store to sell?"

"It was, but I wanted to study it more. Maybe take some better pictures to figure it out." More lying. Would it never end? Please let my nose stay smallish.

"Good thing he didn't bury it in the woods."

"Yeah. Good thing." I slid the cube into my pocket, vowing to dunk it in a bucket of salt water later to see if it helped with its seriously bad vibe. How had I not noticed it before?

"I can't wait until tomorrow night," he stated, grabbing my hands and squeezing them.

"Me too," I squeaked. Gawd, I had so much landscaping to do. And decisions to make. Trimmed Venus, landing strip, or was he the kind to want it all gone? I didn't think I could do that, not after years of thick covering down below.

"The party doesn't start until nine. I'll pick you up about quarter to?"

I blinked at him. Party? It took me a second to realize he must be referring to the one at the mill. "Maybe you want to come over a bit earlier so we can spend some time together?" I heated at the boldness of it. Could I be more obvious I wanted to jump him?

"I'll try. It will depend on a few things."

I struggled to hold in my disappointment. "No worries."

"Don't forget an overnight bag," he teased.

I nodded, not trusting myself to speak.

He leaned in and gave me a soft kiss. "Until tomorrow then."

It seemed too long.

Forever.

Not enough time. What would I wear? What would I pack? He told me to have an overnight bag.

Help!

Since I was too distracted to scrub the floor after Darryl's departure, I set aside my scrubbing brush and called Trish. No answer. Texted Marjorie. Got a short reply: Working. My own fault for cancelling our original shopping trip. My friends made other plans.

Wendy... I hesitated. Did I really want to enlist

my daughter's aid in getting laid? Our relationship hadn't achieved that level yet.

I had no one to help me.

The bell over the door chimed. I'd forgotten to lock it after Darryl left.

Someone came inside, as I said, "Sorry, we're closed."

"That's a good look for you. On your knees."

A tingle went through me, a sense of awareness that bloody well only ever happened with one person.

"Kane."

13

"Hello, sweetheart."

As I popped to my feet, cheeks hot at his innuendo, I wanted to be angry at him. To rail and rant and rave. But I saw that cocky smile, remembered him with his sword.

My guardian. I also wanted to kiss him.

He glanced around. "It's not as bad as it could have been."

"I would have preferred it happen to someone else." I'd had more than my fair share of bad luck.

"I'm sorry, sweetheart." The soft words gave me an urge to get close for a hug, to hear that gravelly voice let me know everything would be all right. Kane, my protector, was here. He'd fix this for me.

I was immediately pissed at myself. A woman didn't need a man to fix things for her. But I could use a friend. Someone who wouldn't think I was crazy when I talked about magic.

"Do you think this is happening because I'm cursed?"

"You do seem to have an unnatural string of luck." Kane stated, glancing around at the sooty walls and shelves of my store.

"Especially with fire. First my house. Marjorie's place. My car. Now this."

"You make it sound targeted."

I rolled my shoulders. "Technically my house and car were." Martin had burned down the first with me in it and then apparently tried to Molotov cocktail my car. This after he chopped down a tree to land on it. "Marjorie's place was classed as an accident caused by candles."

"You think *this* is an accident?" His tone implied a skepticism I shared.

"So far, it appears that way. Murphy says they think it started in the box." He'd told me when he called earlier that day. "It looks as if something sparked inside of it. Which is annoying, given I had someone come in to make sure everything was up to code before I bought the place." I'd gotten the shop for a song. Betsy liked me. Even named a goat after me. Said maybe the bad spirits would be fooled and take it instead of me when the moon bled and the orcs rose to rule.

Again with the orcs. Trish believed in orcs, too, and yet I couldn't find anything about them online other than they were popular villains in video games.

Kane frowned. "No, there was nothing wrong with this box. I had Brigda check this place over when she came to fix the windows."

I glared at him. "You had your lackey snooping?"

"I asked her to make sure the place was safe, especially given the vandalism."

Even then, protecting me. Why? And why not take credit for it earlier? Unless he lied. Except...I didn't think he was.

"Accident or vandalism, my insurance company is freaking." Meaning my premiums would probably hike.

"If you need help, you just have to ask."

"I doubt I'd like your price."

"What if I said it would cost you nothing at all?"

I couldn't help but snort. "I'm sure you'd shove it in my face that I owed you."

"There is only one thing I want to shove in your face."

I gaped at him.

His grin was slow. Mischievous.

Sexy.

"You would make a crude remark. Isn't that just like a man who can't win an argument?"

"And you keep deflecting. It's going to happen."

"Not even if you were the last man on earth, so stop with the desperate attempts to get in my pants." I tossed my hair.

Me.

Tossed my hair.

Holy crap, I was living my own soap opera.

"Sweetheart, you are too much."

"If you don't like it, leave."

Kane laughed. "Never said I didn't enjoy it."

"Why are you here?" I asked. He appeared better today, the pallor gone from his features.

"Just wanted to check on you."

"Kind of late to come to my rescue."

"Are you upset I didn't come sooner? I wanted to," he purred, stepping closer.

"Did your mommy stop you?" I taunted.

Rather than appear angry, amusement creased his features. "You should know better than to think I'd care what someone else wanted."

"Obviously, or you wouldn't keep ignoring my wishes and showing up."

"I show up because I can't help myself."

As words went, they caused a flutter. "Maybe your mother should try reverse psychology."

His smile only widened. "Here's the thing. I know you're bad for me. There is no future for us."

"Obviously since I have no intention of dating you."

"Dating." He snorted. "Is that what you think we'd be doing if we were together?" He stepped closer. His heat circled me, and his nearness had me tilting my head back.

"I'm aware you don't respect me or my boundaries."

"Is that what you think Darryl is doing? Respecting you?" He uttered a short bark of laughter and then turned an intent stare on me. "When I'm with you, the last thing I want to do is take things slow. I want to peel the clothes from you and kiss every inch of your body. I want to bury myself in you and feel you climax on me. With me. Crying out my name. Clawing my back."

With each word, my chest grew tighter and tension coiled inside me. Especially between my legs. God help me, I wanted it, too.

I wanted to be taken with passion as if I were the most desirable thing in the world. Wanted to be one of those women tossed against a wall and ravished. It wouldn't happen since it wasn't Darryl's style.

And I was okay with that. For now.

"You have no idea what I want or like. But you apparently like it a bit violent." I huffed.

"It's called passion, sweetheart."

"My passion is reserved for Darryl."

"Ah yes, your boyfriend. The one you barely see."

How did he know? "Are you spying on me still?"

"Yup."

He didn't even deny it.

"Stop stalking me."

"No."

"You can't say no."

"Just did."

"I'll get a restraining order."

He leaned closer. "Go right ahead, sweetheart. It will just make you more desirable. The forbidden fruit."

"You are so frustrating," I grumped.

"I have something that will fix that." He winked.

I gaped. I wanted to press my thighs so tight I could have pulverized some grapes into wine.

"Is that open mouth an invitation?"

I snapped my jaw shut. "You're impossible to talk to."

"But at least I'm here to talk. Longer than your boyfriend, I hear."

It bothered me that he seemed to know so much about me and my love life. "Did you notice the time he spent alone with me in my bedroom after carrying me from the beach?"

The teasing expression vanished. "Why was he carrying you? Did something happen? Were you attacked?"

"Don't tell me there's something you don't know," I taunted.

"What happened?" Gone was the outrageous Kane, replaced with the seriously intent one.

"It was nothing."

"It's not nothing if they managed to attack you during the day."

I stared at him. "What's daytime got to do with anything?" It hadn't occurred to me that my incidents happened mostly at night. "Wait, if The Chill can only attack at night, does that make it a vampire? It vants to suck my blood." I snickered my way through a bad Count Dracula impression.

"I'm surprised you find this amusing," was his dry response.

"It seems kind of silly. My magic doesn't have

problems with sunlight." I'd done a small spell just that morning to heat the walkway and remove some ice so the house didn't have to exert itself.

"Not all magic is the same."

"What kind do you have?"

"What makes you think I have any?"

"How else would you know so much?"

"I like to read."

Such a simple claim. Too simple. "I do, too, but there don't seem to be any books on the subject."

"There are thousands of books on magic."

"Mostly fiction. Or stuff to toss in a cauldron. None of them cover the sigils."

"Because sigils are a funnel for magic."

"Because it has to have shape," I mumbled aloud.

"Shape. Intent. Focus. Strength."

"Are you a strong warlock?"

His laughter showed off his straight white teeth. "I guess you could call me that. Although my blade work is also quite fine."

"How do you learn to fight with a sword?"

"Very carefully. I'll show you if you'd like."

I almost said yes. Almost fell into his personable trap. "Maybe I'll see if Darryl wants to take lessons with me."

The reminder wiped the mirth from his expression. "Sounds like an excellent idea, given you were attacked."

"Not exactly. I'm thinking I got hit with back-lash when a spell went wrong."

"What did you do?" His voice turned stern.

"Nothing." At his glare, I amended with, "Just drew one of the symbols I'd seen in Grandma's book. It was just supposed to help me remember. I wanted to see if I'd forgotten anything in my past." Because the more I tried to peek at my childhood, the more I noticed the holes in it.

"You cast a spell of recall using what parameters?"

"Say what?" Because I had no idea what he spoke of.

"Magic needs to be bound. In your case, a combination of sigil and intent."

"Um. I drew the symbol." But I didn't know what he meant by the latter.

Kane frowned. "And then activated it without setting up specific guidance?"

"So that's bad?" I said in a tiny voice.

"With no instruction, your spell will end up in a loop that siphons magic to feed it until it combusts, usually killing the caster."

"I didn't die."

"Then you were lucky. An unbound spell of

recollection might have brought you back to the dawn of time and exploded your mind."

"Well, it didn't, and I don't remember a single thing." I shrugged even as his words niggled. Something had happened to me. I just couldn't recall what exactly. His revelation begged the question, "How do you know all this?" And why did the one guy I was trying to keep away from have all the answers?

"I was taught."

"By who?"

"No one you will ever meet."

"Then how am I supposed to learn?" Because while I'd assumed magic should be handled with caution, my experience the previous day proved as a warning that it could have deadly consequence.

"Your grandmother was supposed to teach you."

"Obviously she didn't." Or I'd forgotten. "You could show me."

Showing a rare reluctance, Kane shoved his hands into his pockets. "I can't."

"Why not? You said you'd teach me sword fighting. How is this any different?" I expected him to make a crude demand. He'd teach me in exchange for sex. Kane was outrageous in that respect.

"I can't because I've already betrayed enough for you."

"What's that supposed to mean? Is this about your mother again? Because your family hates me?"

"It would be easier if I could hate you. Then I could accomplish the task that I've been training my entire life for without regret."

It was the most cryptic thing he'd ever said, and chillingly honest, judging by the bleakness in his gaze.

"Is this about me not selling my property again? Is the company putting pressure on you to close the deal?" His family had many business interests in the world, acquiring property being one of them.

He cupped my chin, running a thumb over my jaw, his stare intent. "It was never about land, only ever about you. But you made your choice. And it wasn't me."

"It was never going to be you and me." No matter how he made my pulse pound. There was something dark about Kane. Raw. Violent.

A part of me waited for him to kiss me. Another wanted a reason to shove him away.

Instead, he gave me a sad smile and said, "*Au revoir, mon amour.*" The French equivalent of, "Farewell, my beloved."

I must have misunderstood.

14

By early afternoon, I had a list. A massive list that spawned baby lists, who had little lists of their own. I'd compartmentalized the things I had to do and buy to get my business up and going again. I had a plan.

A plan could be the mightiest tool of all.

It involved a lot of phone calls to order services, mostly shut down until January second. But I got appointments made in between my shower, petting my cat, and getting dressed to go shopping. I still needed underwear and a dress.

Trish finally answered her phone.

"Hey."

"Hi." My best friend sounded out of breath.

"Sorry our shopping trip got messed up," I said with a laugh that lacked any kind of sincere mirth.

"Totally understandable."

"Thanks for finding me on the ice."

"Bad enough we lost your grandmother to the cold. We couldn't lose you, too."

We? Weird choice of words. "I don't suppose you're available today?"

"Hold on a second." The pure silence of the mute button meant she was discussing it with someone else. Mostly likely Marjorie. I wondered at the secrecy though. Did they already have plans? Was I intruding?

Trish returned. "I've got until supper time. Then Jojo and I are meeting with another couple for dinner."

"Oh." I'd not known they had other friends, which sounded horrible even in my own head. Of course, they did. The fact I didn't have many didn't mean everyone sucked at building a circle of companions.

"We'd invite you, but it's couples euchre night."

The explanation didn't help. It just reminded me of Kane's words. How Darryl didn't spend much time with me. He'd been scarce since Boxing Day—the day after Christmas.

"That's fine. I suck at cards." I'd not played since college. Martin and I used to until the kids came along.

"Meet you at the Pink Lace Don't Tell store at the mall in thirty minutes?"

"Sure." I hung up and sighed.

I needed to not let everything be so personal with me. Needed to stop second-guessing motives and perceiving slights that didn't exist.

Maybe Darryl and I could have our own couple thing, like bowling night, or we could train Herbie to do dog shows. The thought of that ginormous, gangly dog wearing a bow and prancing around was enough to make me smile as I headed out.

Maybe I'd pop by Darryl's place on the way back just to say hi.

It took me just under thirty minutes to arrive at the mall, meaning I was already browsing when Trish joined me. My cheeks felt hot. It was too hot. I think I was having a hot flash in the store.

"Please don't tell me you're going to wear black. The popping of your widow cherry deserves something joyous for the occasion," Trish declared as she waded the racks of provocative underwear.

"I'm not a virgin," I reminded her, sifting quickly past the scrap of fabric with the hole in the butt. I planned to start with the basics, which meant front and back covered.

"You were with one man for more than twenty years. One. Man," Trish said with a shudder.

"And? You telling me you're not planning to be with Marjorie forever?"

"Yes. But the plan is to build a stable of dildos, one for each letter of the alphabet to make sure we keep changing things up."

I had nothing to say. Literally nothing. I had a purple pocket rocket bought at the pharmacy because hey, if they sold it, it must be healthy for me. The idea of a stable… It had merit.

"Don't look at me like that," Trish exclaimed. "I'll have you know a properly made phallus will never disappoint. Even without batteries they can still do the job."

"But they can't hug you after. Or share popcorn while watching a scary movie."

"Good point, which is why it is time for you to lustily go after what you want."

She was talking about me and Darryl. "Why do you think I'm here?" I fingered a pair of pink satin panties with a bold pattern of flowers.

"I'm surprised you haven't taken him for a test run yet."

"We're taking things slow. Waiting for the right time."

"The sooner you pop that hesitant cherry, the better. You'll feel better."

"I feel fine." If slightly nauseous.

"You'll feel finer after."

I laughed. "That isn't even a word." But I understood the sentiment.

"Try these on." Trish plucked several garments and handed them to me. Most were not the type I would have dared contemplate.

"You need me to help you get into them?" Trish asked with an exaggerated wink.

"And have your girlfriend kill me?" I shook my head. Not to mention, no one had seen my body in a long time, unless my family doctor counted.

The inside of the dressing room was spacious enough to spread out. I removed my purse and clothes and left them folded on the bench. I did my best to avoid looking in the mirror. I'd kept my underpants on because I wasn't putting on any bottoms without anything there, but my breasts hung heavily. I hated them but stuffed them into a bra and straightened.

I usually stuck to sports bras. Easy to stow and forget the boobs, but the contraption I wore—made of stiff fabric and wire—did something to my breasts. Lifted them and shaped them into something that made smile.

I'd had nice boobs in my twenties. This bra took twenty years off my current set. It made me wonder if I should make an appointment and talk to a plastic surgeon. Research showed lots of women my age opting for some work. I could certainly use it on my stomach.

My cotton undies went up to the waist and covered the loose skin bulge. I slid some panties over mine, the crinkle of the paper in the crotch making me think of a pad. They sat bikini style on my hips. The sideways profile had me tearing them off quick. Nope. All the tinier scraps ended up being a no. But I did like the boy shorts in lace, tight enough to hold everything in, and a hole on the bottom for access. Which made me blush so hot I thought I'd pass out.

Once I got over my embarrassment, I liked that they could stay on and I wouldn't have any jiggly bits if things got vigorous.

Oh gawd.

Just in case I changed my mind when I got home, I bought a second set of bottoms, fully sewn shut.

As for the dress, we went with an empire waist round neck and half sleeves. The skirt flared around my knees, and in the mirror, I couldn't help but smile at the hourglass shape.

"I love it." I twirled left then right.

"It's flattering and has easy access," Trish declared with satisfaction.

"I just wish we didn't have to go to the party."

"You have to go."

"I'd rather spend it with Darryl at his place, or mine." Just him and me.

"Where's the fun in that?"

I could think of plenty.

Trish and I split up at the food court. Her to go home to get ready for dinner and card night. Me, I had a salad with grilled chicken and daydreamed about my New Year's Eve date.

We'd go to the party and dance, kiss at midnight, and then he'd take me home.

No, his home where there weren't any kids.

We'd make love in front of his fireplace.

Wait, I didn't know if he had one. Didn't matter, we'd make love, and I'd wake up to him touching me. Sliding into me from behind like they did in the romance books.

I couldn't wait. It would be just the start of sleepovers. Which had me biting my lip. I'd bought a few sets of matching lingerie, but I'd neglected a nightgown. I dropped off my bags at the car and back to the store I went. A big girl who didn't need a friend in order to choose something slutty to wear for her boyfriend.

I settled on trying three different styles, the baby doll one being my top favorite. As I did the shuffle to ditch my clothes and put on the first sexy lace gown, I heard the changing room door beside me slam shut and then two voices.

"I'm not even sure I should bother buying any lingerie. He told me that after spending time with her, he likes to see my perfection."

"How long before he can stop the charade with her?"

"Not until it's all done. He doesn't want to mess anything up."

I wouldn't deny I listened to the sordid tale. A mistress waiting for her lover to leave his wife. Would he? Martin had.

"I don't know how he does it. She's so old and hideous."

"He hates it so much he's extra ardent," boasted the mistress.

"Are you seeing him tonight?"

"Yeah. We're meeting at his station."

I froze at the words. She could mean any number of places. Fire station. Police even. It seemed unlikely she spoke of the gas one.

Still, my paranoia made her words about me. Me and Darryl. Not true of course. I was hardly a wife he couldn't leave.

I bought the tamest nightgown and fled. Prepared myself to drive straight home when I saw the gas station sign ahead. Before I knew it, I'd slowed down, searching for Darryl's truck. It wasn't there.

A part of me sighed. I kept going and gave in to my earlier impulse. I turned on to the road that would take me to Darryl's place.

The gravel drive to his house was packed with cars. The family situation he was obviously dealing with. Had someone died? Shit, I did not want to walk in on that kind of family matter.

I stopped midway up the line of them and started to reverse.

As I reached the road, I had to pause; a vehicle was passing. Before it cleared, I heard a honk.

A glance in front of me showed a blue pickup, and Darryl getting out of the front seat.

15

WHAT SEEMED LIKE A CUTE POP IN FOR A HELLO had just turned tragically wrong. He would think I was crazy, driving out to his place and not stopping in, now staring at him like a deer in headlights about to get murdered. As he leaned down to peer through my window, I lowered it. Waited for him to ask me why I was being so creepy stalkerish.

Instead he smiled. "Naomi. What a pleasure to see you."

"I chickened out," I blurted out. "I saw all the cars and…"

"I've got a few guests, as you can see."

"For how long?"

"Awhile."

There went my New Year's Eve fantasy

involving his plaid couch. "I'm sorry. I should have called or texted before coming over."

"Don't be silly. I'm always happy to see you. Just right now is a little busy."

"I get it. I do." I didn't actually because he'd not really explained anything. Surely, he would when he had the time.

"I was actually going in to work," he said.

I tried to not remember what that woman said. "Oh. You meeting someone?"

"Ha. Only if it's called a misbehaving register."

I could have slapped myself for being suspicious. "That sucks."

"It gets me out of the house for a few minutes. I can't wait until tomorrow night," he said.

His words eased something inside me. "Me, too."

"Later." He tapped the side of my car and stood.

No kiss. I was admittedly a little surprised and disappointed. Then again, we probably had an audience.

I made it home and ran my stuff upstairs like it was candy contraband in my teens. My grandmother hated me eating that processed crap. She called it poison.

I tossed my things onto the bed and stretched.

Body parts popped. Getting old sucked. Every year, something didn't work like it used to. Especially the joints. They made noises now. Sometimes ached when a storm was coming.

My phone beeped, and I dove for my purse on the bed. I juggled it, saw a notification about my lives being replenished for a game, and dropped it. Only as I scrambled on the floor to find it under the bed did my fingers touch the box.

Martin's box.

Which was supposed to be in the trunk of my car.

How had it gotten back inside? And more importantly, when would I burn it?

I pulled it out and glanced at the second-to-last journal. Not the one he kept in prison but the one before he walked out. It started two years ago.

It didn't prove hard to find out when he met his mistress. To see how he went from middle-aged man feeling guilty about cheating on his wife to full-blown adulterer who saw his wife as getting in the way of his happiness.

Helena understands me.

The statement oddly hurt. I'd understood Martin once upon a time. We'd been best friends and partners. We just grew apart, and instead of finding our way back, he moved on with someone else.

Then tried to kill me. I had to wonder if the idea came from him.

Helena says I shouldn't have to share everything I earned. I worked for it. It's mine.

The ramblings continued in that vein and then stopped the day before he came to find me in Canada. The last line being:

It ends now.

I shoved the box under the bed again and, suddenly restless, threw on my snow gear and went for a walk. As usual, it led me to the lake and an oddity in the center of it.

A dark spot. As if the ice were melted and the water seeped through.

Weird. Maybe a bunch of fish peed in the same place. Or a gas was released. Maybe an alien craft crashed.

Which was to say it could be anything. I wasn't a biologist or whatever. I was sure I could find a hundred professionals if I posted the question on social media.

Whatever the reason for the hole, I chalked it up to my lake being special. I knelt and placed my hand on the ice. The snow had been swept clean in some spots. I could have sworn I felt a faint hum.

The hair on my neck prickled as if I were being watched.

I stood and turned, eyeing the strip of forest between me and the cottage. The shoreline was empty. Nothing moved, and yet the sense of not being alone persisted.

I stared until the cold bit through my clothes before heading back to the house.

"SHE KNOWS YOU'RE WATCHING." HIS LOVER SPOKE as if he cared to hear her words. She'd failed in her attempt at controlling the source and now thought to cater favor with Leviathan, the chosen one.

The raven he possessed was perched at the very top of a tree and struggling. It didn't want to be there. The protections on the land made it itch to move away.

He knew the feeling. Each time Leviathan visited, he just wanted to leave. It hurt to be that close. It disgusted him to have to pretend with her.

"She might know, but she can't stop anything. Not now. Not this close." He'd finally gotten things where they needed to be.

"You should have bedded her by now. Cemented your position."

"There have been complications."

"There's a pill for that, you know." She mocked, and he retaliated by grabbing her by the hair. Dragging her closc.

"Do I need to remind you of my virility?"

"Yes, please." Her pupils dilated. Pleasure parted her lips. She ran her finger down his chest.

"Don't be greedy. You know I need my energy for tomorrow."

She didn't take offense. She licked her lips and smiled. "Are you sure she's going to cooperate?"

"She doesn't have a choice." By submission or force, he would bind the witch to him.

16

I woke on New Year's Eve way too early. I couldn't help myself. I was a mess of nerves.

For distraction, I spent some time in my shop, removing the things I knew were trash. Affixing the sign I'd printed that read, Closed for Repairs.

I had lunch at the diner counter. Orville only peeked from the kitchen briefly. He didn't come out. It bothered me. He'd been gruff before but always nice to me. Had I done something to earn his displeasure? Marjorie had said something about him seeing someone.

Speaking of whom, Marjorie wasn't there, nor did I know the four waitresses bustling around. A room full of people and I felt alone. The bowl in front of me held a Greek salad with grilled chicken. Green and healthy. It would be tangy and salty because of the feta cheese. A nice meal that crunched in my mouth and only increased the sadness in me that told me I should have cake.

I deserved that spoonful of sugar, more carbs in one bite than my lifestyle allowed in a day. It would taste too sweet. But I'd have another. And another. Stuffing my face until I ate way more than I should and my stomach hurt. I'd be bloated and slightly nauseous. I'd want to nap.

The litany of bad things helped me curb the craving. Only barely. Then the ultimate distraction sat down beside me, filling the just vacated stool at the counter.

My Kane-sense tingled. Don't look. I wouldn't look. Maybe I was mistaken and just hyper-paranoid. Maybe it wasn't Kane.

I glanced over. My heart did a funny jump. When I felt myself wanting to smile, I tamped it down to mutter a grouchy, "Still following me?" I should be pissed he invaded my privacy like that, but there was a part of me that enjoyed the attention. Kane might confuse me on too many levels, but with him constantly coming around, I never felt forgotten.

"Seems kind of conceited to assume I'm here because of you," he drawled. "Did it ever occur to you I come for the excellent fish and chips?"

"You look more like the steak and risotto that ends in a cigar with a brandy type."

Kane always appeared well put together. Distinguished without going overboard.

"I'm a man of many appetites, sweetheart. Not that you'll ever know."

The reply brought an unladylike noise to my lips. "Are you trying reverse psychology to get me to jump in your bed?"

"Not anymore, sweetheart. You clearly have your panties set on Darryl, which I don't understand. He wins. I lose. Good luck with your choice."

"You're giving up?" It should have elated me. Disappointment might have lined my query.

"Would you prefer I didn't?" He leaned against the counter, his entire attention on me. It occurred to me that in the past few days, I'd had longer conversations with him than Darryl.

Which only went to prove I'd been seeing him too often. If Kane gave up, that would stop. No more distractions or outrageous propositions.

I didn't understand why it bothered me. "What are your plans for tonight?" I turned the conversation in another direction and took a stab at my salad.

"If I tell you I have a date, will you throw a jealous fit?"

The fork in my hand bent. Cheap metal that didn't last against my anger.

Why? I shouldn't give a fuck. Seriously. I shouldn't, yet at the idea of him and someone else... holy jealousy followed by anger. Player. Kane the fucking player, acting all hot for me one minute, and two seconds later he was already making plans with someone else... "Why would I care if you're dating? I say good. It will keep you out of my hair."

"Glad to hear it, because my date and I will probably see you and your boyfriend at the party."

"You're going to the mill?" A dumb question given he was part owner.

"I don't think there's a single person in town who isn't," was his reply.

Meaning no way I'd miss seeing him there with his date. "See you there."

The light in the diner sizzled. A tremor went through my seat. The noise in the place exploded a few decibels. The person just behind me complained loudly his phone just died with an eighty-five-percent battery.

I speared my salad.

"I didn't think you needed to murder vegetables to eat them," was the murmur by my ear.

A shiver went through me.

I turned my head and held my breath. He was

close to me. Close enough I could see the gold and rusty flakes in the depths of Kane's eyes. Smell his cologne. The nearness of him did something unholy and decadent to my pussy. I throbbed. In public.

The urge to kiss him was insane. I could see why when drunk I might have given in to the temptation. There was something about Kane. Something that drew me despite everything.

Desire churned and urged me to lean forward and kiss him. I wasn't drunk this time. How would it feel? I doubted it would be the sweetness I got with Darryl. With Kane, wantonness drove me. As if I were drugged.

Or bespelled.

I jerked back. "You're using magic on me."

"I am talking to you."

"You're seducing me with your words," I accused. "You did the same thing that night at the bar."

"That night in the bar you were drunk."

"My friends think you slipped me a mickey."

"Drugged you?" He laughed. "That wasn't me. You were showing signs of slurring before we ever spoke."

"So you admit you knew I wasn't myself yet took me outside and took advantage of me."

"First of all, you asked me to take you outside for some fresh air."

"Then you proceeded to maul me."

"Maul you?" He sounded so surprised. "Do you really not remember your greedy hands all over my body? You were the one kissing me. My back was against the car because you had me pinned there."

"Now I know you're lying. I'm not aggressive like that." I only had fuzzy memories of that night. Most of it reconstructed based on what Trish told me. She hated Kane, though. Would she have lied to get him in trouble?

"You took charge of that kiss. Was it any wonder I gave in?"

Staring at him, I did remember. I recalled my hands fisting his shirt as I leaned against him outside. My blood boiled, and I rode his thigh, humping it.

My memory had him cupping my face, holding me and saying, "Slow down."

I didn't want to slow down, though. I'd wanted him to do something about the ache in me.

Then Trish arrived and tore me away. I blinked at him. "You're a good kisser." The words fell out of my mouth, and I couldn't take them back.

His lips curved, but rather than something arrogant, he said, "Did you think the attraction between us was one sided?"

Looking at him, I had a hard time believing he was that attracted to me. "I think you're playing me."

"To what end?"

"You want me to dump Darryl. To hurt him. Because you hate him."

"Hate?" He shook his head as he leaned away to his own space. "It is more complicated than that."

Had he just admitted he used me as part of a vendetta?

"I don't want to see you anymore."

"You won't. Consider this our goodbye." He slid off the stool and left.

I stared at my bowl of salad. A great big soggy hunk of sadness. My gaze strayed to the chocolate cake, thick with icing. I tossed money down and ran out of there.

My encounter with Kane frazzled me. Especially since I saw it in a different light. If Kane had never drugged me or assaulted me, then I'd been hating him for the wrong reasons.

Not that it mattered now. Even if I didn't have Darryl, I still wouldn't date Kane. He was crude and stubborn. For all that he'd saved me that one night in the woods, I still didn't trust him.

And why was I even still thinking about it? Darryl was the man for me. A simple, hardworking guy who treated me with respect. Hopefully a little less respect tonight.

Once I got home I did my filial duty by checking on Geoff, who was planning a night of gaming with his online friends. Mother guilt hit me, and I offered to cancel my plans. He refused, whereupon I profusely apologized until he yelled at me to go get ready and stop trying to chicken out.

Me, a coward?

Damned right I was. My stomach had a stampeding herd of butterflies that made me want to throw up. Should a first date feel like morning sickness?

I wanted this. I couldn't wait. I was just nervous. It would be fine. People went on dates every day. I could do this. It wouldn't kill me.

I fled to my room and got prepping.

In my younger days, it took minutes. A bit of gloss, dark blue shadow and eyeliner, a quick shave, and hair shoved in a sideways high pony. In my forties it involved more prep, and I was glad I'd recently sprung for a pedicure. Marjorie had insisted in case my feet ended up around someone's neck. I didn't think I was that bendy, but I did like my red toes.

I drew the line at being waxed. That kind of pain just wasn't my style. No, apparently, I preferred to sit in my tub, leg hauled up on the side, cramp in my other thigh, so I could squint and hunt for those pesky dark hairs around my ankle that could grow an inch overnight. I removed every single follicle I could reach.

Since I wasn't sure what the status was on fuzzy

thighs, I shaved those, too. My pits got taken down to the skin, and I grimaced at the shadow my roots left. If I wasn't a pussy for pain, I'd wax them.

I left the dreaded bush for last. I eyed the thatch, wiry and strong. The collagen I took in my coffee didn't just strengthen and thicken the hair on my head.

I performed a test swipe where my thigh creased against my pubes and the thin border of my pelt. The blades clogged. I'd need more powerful help.

"Got any clippers?" I asked aloud. Perhaps the house kept a set of garden shears nearby.

Thump.

The noise came from the cupboard under the sink.

I eyed it. Demon in hiding waiting to spring or the house providing? Just in case it was the first, I grabbed the toilet paper rack—the kind that held multiple rolls—and brandished it as I reached for the cupboard.

Opening it, I squeaked, "Not funny!"

The house had managed to wedge a weed whacker in there. I swear I felt it shake in mirth.

"It is not that bushy," I grumbled. Total lie. It was a jungle down there.

When I turned around, the stool by the tub held a regular shaver with an attachment. With much cursing, contorting, and a hairy murder scene in the tub by the time I was done, I managed to tame the locks down below to a sleek pelt. I wouldn't do a full-on shave, mostly because I feared it would rash before I got to the main event.

I had to shower to make sure I got all of the residue off. Then I moisturized. Face. Body. Feet. Even my girl parts got a bit of pampering, so they'd smell pretty.

Then came the tucking of my boobs and belly into my underwear. I wasn't model perfect, but I was pleased with what I saw. I cocked a hip and posed. Even blew a kiss.

I wasn't too old to be sexy.

Next came the hair, which I'd been getting into the habit of blow drying every other day and keeping it nicely shaped and colored. All part of the new me. Looking good made me feel good. For tonight, I added more than the light mascara and gloss I'd adopted. I dabbed a bit of blush to my cheeks. Some sparkle to my eyes.

A sultry stranger looked back at me in the mirror. I couldn't wait for Darryl to see me.

When the doorbell rang, my heart stopped, and I had a moment of panic. Tonight was the night.

Trish was right. It did feel like I was losing my virginity all over again.

I skipped down the stairs to find Geoff at the door, Grisou by his side. The cat who sometimes thought he was a guard dog. The pair stared at Darryl, grilling him.

"So," my son drawled, "you're taking my mom out. I'll expect her home before dawn. And no drinking and driving."

"Geoffrey!" I yelped his name and blushed, which drew masculine laughter.

Darryl peeked at me around my son and whistled. "You look amazing."

The compliment only made me bubble with happiness. I couldn't help but blush. "Thank you." Had he noticed I'd worn the brooch he'd given me for Christmas?

"I can't wait to show you off." As I slid on my boots, Darryl said to Geoff, "Don't worry. I'll take good care of Naomi."

I hoped so. Really *good* care.

He helped me into my coat then out to his truck.

Only once he climbed in the driver side did I exclaim, "I forgot my overnight bag."

Darryl winked as he said, "You won't be needing any clothes for what I have planned."

"Oh." A hot exclamation that went with my

surely red cheeks. "But what about the people at your house?"

"We won't be going back to my house."

Had he rented us a hotel room? Romantic. Tawdry. Nerve wracking. Holy moly, it was going to happen.

The conversation was light on the drive over. Me mostly babbling about the shop, and even the damned cat. When we stopped, I was surprised to see us parked at the front of the mill given the packed lot.

"Aren't you afraid you'll get towed?"

"They wouldn't dare tonight." He offered me a hand to get out of the truck. He grabbed me and slid me down his body. The thrill was cheap and cheek heating. I smiled at him and got one back.

"Shall we go inside?" he said, holding my hand to lead me into the mill.

It appeared almost majestic with thousands of small lights giving it a grandeur it lacked in the reality of day. Overhead, a bright moon shone. The papers claimed we'd see a rare red moon, expected to reach its peak of color around midnight, when the New Year began. I wondered what kind of omen it portended, good or the end of everything, as one newspaper had been claiming of late.

"I wonder why the mill invited the whole town,"

I said as we followed other couples toward the main doors.

"So that everyone might see the fulfillment of a dream years in the making."

Puzzling. I'd not known Darryl was that caught up in the doings of the mill.

I didn't ponder it long, as, just inside, he removed my coat and held me steady as I switched my boots to shoes. Those at least I'd managed to bring, but only because I slipped them into the pockets earlier. I'd worried I'd forget indoor shoes and spend the evening in my Sherpa-lined suede winter boots.

No heels, because I wanted to remain upright, but even if they were simple, I felt like the belle of the ball with my handsome beau. Darryl had dressed up, wearing a mauve silk button-up shirt, paired with an ashy gray coat and pants. He made it unique with the bolero and cowboy boots.

I hugged his arm, so happy I could burst.

Inside the mill, I oohed and aahed at the transformation achieved by lights and streamers strung all over. In the massive room, which I'd recently seen housing bottles and crates, were people. More people than I'd ever imagined could live in town. They gathered in clusters, talking, dancing, drinking, eating. I'd swear they all kept looking my way.

I clutched at Darryl as a hint of panic filled me. Too many bodies in a room too small. I tugged at his arm. "Can we go outside for a minute? I'm feeling a little claustrophobic."

"It's freezing out there. Here. Use this to calm down." As a waiter bearing a large tray with drinks passed, Darryl snared a glass and pressed it into my hand. The liquid was golden and clear. Champagne? Wine? Before I could figure it out, I realized Darryl held a glass, too.

"Aren't you driving?" I asked as he downed it quick.

"Don't worry about that. Drink," he urged me, even as he snared another.

I wanted to say something. Clarify how we'd be getting to a hotel or home. What if he got angry? Could be he had a romantic plan that involved us having a limo pick us up? I might ruin the surprise and my chances if I got all pissy about him having a few drinks. Surely Darryl wouldn't do anything irresponsible that could get us both killed.

"Happy New Year's Eve," I said, lifting my glass in a salute.

He clanged it. "To the new era."

A strange thing to say and yet I heard it over and over as we toured the room. Perhaps some kind of local mantra. Of more interested was Darryl. He strutted across the mill floor as if he owned it, stopping to talk to more people than I ever imagined anyone knowing. Introducing me to everyone. Full name. Naomi Rousseau. It got me more curious stares than I liked.

But it did please me to know he wasn't ashamed to be seen with the town witch. Talk about a difference from when we first met.

An hour into the party, I caught a glimpse of Winnie in a corner, dressed in a silver sheath. It had been a few days since I'd seen her. She'd not been by the house while I was home, so I resorted to leaving a dorky message on her voicemail—*'Hey Winnie, it's your mom, just wanted to wish you a happy New Year's eve. Call me.'* She didn't. Probably busy with her new beau.

I hurried to say hi, ditching Darryl ,who was off to the side whispering with a crony.

A smile tugged my lips. "Winnie! I didn't know you were coming. You look so pretty."

She saw me and froze before giving me a tight smile. "Hey, Mom."

"Long time, no see. Is everything okay? Are you here with your new friend?" I glanced around, wondering who her date was.

"Yeah." She fidgeted. "Listen, we need to talk.

There are things you don't know. Things I have to tell you."

"Is this about the book of spells you ruined?"

Her lips flattened.

"Why did you wreck it? Surely you could have—"

She cut me off. "There's so much you don't understand."

"Then tell me."

"I can't. It's complicated." She hesitated before saying in a rush, "You're in—"

"Evening, Naomi." Jace slid in close behind my daughter. Too close. His hand on her waist made my gaze narrow.

Jace and Winnie. To my relief I didn't feel any jealousy, even if Jace was an attractive guy more my age. But I was annoyed. What was Winnie thinking getting involved with another older guy? On the heels of the ire came the hurt. Not only did Winnie keep it a secret, she'd been next door this entire time and not once popped in to see me.

Why?

"I told you she'd be judgy about it," my daughter muttered to Jace.

In that one statement I knew why she'd kept it a secret. Because her new boyfriend was a man old enough to date me. A man I'd had a few lusty thoughts about. But Jace had chosen someone else, just like I was with someone else.

"Congratulations on getting together. That's awesome. Really, I'm so happy. With you next door, we'll be able to visit whenever we want. It will be great for grandkids." I wanted to slap myself, I certainly mentally winced as I proceeded to go overboard in how okay it was that my early-twenties daughter was dating a guy almost twice her age. Apparently, I wasn't as progressive as I liked to think.

"Mom!" Winnie exclaimed. "Why must you be like this?"

Maybe because I'd seen her make bad choices before? "How long?" I asked.

"Not long. We wanted to tell you."

But feared my reaction. Great. Tiptoe around the midlife psychotic widow.

"There you are. I've been looking for you." Darryl's purr tickled me as he tugged me close. I'd never been happier to be rescued.

"Let's dance," I demanded, turning into him, seeking the distraction of his allure.

"I would love to," he drawled.

Lucky me, the music slowed as we got onto the area designated as a dance floor. It was dark enough that I could cling tight to Darryl as we rocked in a circle. His hands were on my hips, mine on his shoulders, head on his chest, eyes closed. When I did open them, it was to see only Darryl and I were dancing in the time-honored circle. The rest of the people did magic with movement. Couples weaved and dipped, a seamless synchronicity that mesmerized. Swoop. Twirl. Bow.

How did they move in time? It was the kind of thing that took hours, months, of practice.

It enthralled me. Filled me. Energized me.

The song ended, and Darryl pushed a drink into my hands. I was hot. Flushed. I gulped it, but the sweetness didn't quench. I set it down, more than half full, and danced again, glued to Darryl. Rubbing against him wantonly. It might have been shameful if everyone else wasn't doing it, too.

Inhibitions were lowered, and I was one of them. Running my fingers through his hair. Grinding myself against him. So hot he could have dragged me off to a corner and I would not have protested.

Midnight drew close, and I decided I should freshen up.

"I need to use the ladies' room."

"Of course." He escorted me to the swinging doors that led to the hall with the washrooms. "I'll wait here for you."

"Hopefully there's no line," I quipped. Giddy, I almost skipped into the bathroom. I did my business, listening as people entered and left in a steady stream.

I emerged and washed my hands. As I dried them on a paper towel, I clued into a conversation between stalls.

"I don't know how he's doing it. He usually only has the most beautiful women in his bed."

"It's got to be killing him to fake it. She's gross," was the higher-pitched reply. It was shades of the lingerie store all over again.

"I wonder if he'll close his eyes when he has to fuck her."

I almost gasped at the cruelty of their words. I wondered who they spoke of because, quite honestly, the majority of people at the party were gorgeous.

The toilets flushed as I hurried to toss the paper towel away. Then a stall door opened before I could leave and a woman a bit younger than me with silver hair pinned atop her head stared at me, eyes wide. The stall beside ejected a shorter woman with a platinum pixie cut.

"Hi," I muttered as I stepped past. No reply. I shoved through the exit, but the door hadn't shut when I heard a shocked, "She's even worse looking up close."

"No wonder he's getting so drunk."

That was definitely about me, and it kicked me in the gut. I leaned against the wall to steady myself.

Bitches.

They were obviously catty and jealous that Darryl chose me. I clung to that desperately as a lifeline, but their barbs struck home and burrowed into that insecure part of me that still existed. Was I good enough?

I knew my shortcomings. The crinkles at the corners of my eyes and around my lips, the gray in my hair hidden by my hairdresser. But every woman my age had those. I couldn't stop getting older. Just like I could do nothing for below the neck where the weight loss and change in body shape left flabby bits behind.

Darryl would be the first man in more than twenty years to see me in all my glory and faults. He'd touch skin ravaged by pregnancy and weight and age.

I wanted to be sick. What if he didn't like what he saw? What if he couldn't get an erection like Martin my ex? Martin had claimed I was the reason he couldn't get hard and didn't want sex.

What if... What if those women were right?

What if they're just bitches and I'm being old Naomi? Old Naomi let other people decide her self-worth. Old Naomi didn't feel good enough and thought people hated her.

What did I care what two twats thought about me? I was here with Darryl because he wanted to be with me.

I couldn't let anxiety, fueled by alcohol, take me down any dark paths. No more booze.

As I emerged from the hallway, I glanced to see the party in full swing. Darryl still stood where I'd left him.

He smiled at me. No one else. That meant something.

I tried to find that bubble of happiness from before, only I couldn't relax. My gaze darted around the room, and I would have sworn I saw eyes upon us, judging and disdainful. Lips twisted in disgust.

It had to be the booze. I was getting paranoid. My anxiety was obviously exacerbated by the amount of people and alcohol. I just needed to sober up.

About ten minutes before midnight, I left his side, telling him I needed to use the bathroom again. As I splashed water on my face, I told myself to stop being stupid. It was almost midnight. I should be in Darryl's arms, preparing to kiss him.

I exited the bathroom and glanced up the hall toward the party. The noise. The music. The crushing heat. I knew what I needed. A few minutes in the fresh air. The far end of the hall had a door marked exit.

That was exactly what I needed. I headed for it and pushed the waist-high, metal bar to swing it open. I stepped outside. The door hung in place. I'd hate to be locked out.

I stepped outside, and the cold night air surrounded me. Bathed my flushed skin. Filled my lungs. I took a step and then another down the short flight of stairs, hitting the ground and hugging myself.

Already I felt better. Clearer. It might have been relaxing if the door hadn't closed.

18

I stared in utter disbelief at the stupid door. Apparently, it was on some kind of timer, because it shut all by itself. With no handle on the outside, it couldn't be opened. Talk about a dumb design.

I'd have to see if I could get someone's attention. Was anyone in the hall? Rapid tapping and then a press of my ear on the door didn't net me a rescuer. I'd have to go around.

I'd almost made it to the corner when I heard some voices.

A female purred, "You poor thing. Once you've done your duty, come see me. I'll make you forget her."

I froze rather than round the corner and step past the lovers. Good thing, too, because the next voice froze me.

"I'll be thinking of you as I'm fucking her. Maybe you should give me a hand to get me started," was Darryl's reply.

I died in that moment. Completely and utterly shattered.

Darryl wasn't into me. Then why the charade? Why pretend?

I knew the sounds of kissing, and still I couldn't walk away. "I have to go," he said. "It's almost midnight."

"Think of me when you kiss her."

"I already do."

I bit my fist lest I make a sound. I hurt. Bad. I was also really freaking cold. I wanted my coat and boots, but I couldn't go inside. Couldn't face him. Anyone.

Why? Why would he do this to me?

The voices disappeared, and despite my garb, I hunched my shoulders and marched into the parking lot, wishing the lights were less bright. My anger wouldn't keep me warm for long. Maybe I could find someone to hitch a ride with.

Or I could call someone. I had my purse and my phone. Geoff would come get me. As I kept marching, I dug into the bag. A clutch purse that didn't have much room. It also didn't have my phone.

Seriously?

"Argh!" I threw the purse, scattering my gloss and identification, as if anyone would have carded me for booze. "Can't I get a break?" I screamed to the sky, tears rolling down my cheeks. I scrubbed at them even as I wondered, now what?

"What happened, sweetheart?" A rustle from a shadow between two cars turned into Kane, a cigarette dangling from his fingers.

"Since when do you smoke?" Stupid thing to say, but flustered, I tried to pretend nonchalance.

"When I'm stressed, which is a lot more often these days." He tossed the glowing butt. "You haven't said why you're out here, no boots or coat."

"Because you were right. I'm a shitty judge of character."

"What did Darryl do?"

"Let's just say he's not the man I thought he was." I couldn't look at Kane and glanced down spotting the brooch Darryl gave me. I couldn't remove it fast enough and I threw it, not wanting it anywhere near me.

"Is this the wrong time to say I told you so?

"You were right." My words tasted of lemony bitterness. I began marching past him, no idea how I'd walk miles to town but so fucking sick of it all.

"Where are you going?"

"Somewhere that isn't here."

"You'll freeze. Get back inside."

"No. I'd rather take my chances with winter." Probably the dumbest, most emotional thing I'd said, which was why I sighed. "Where's your car?"

He pointed. We were leaning on it.

"You can't leave," he said. "It's almost midnight."

"And? Another day, more bullshit. You were so right. And I knew better. Knew..." The words faded off in defeat. Would I add whining to the list of my failures?

"Ah, sweetheart." Kane pulled me close, and I was hurting enough to allow it. He stroked my hair, drawing me into the warmth he exuded. "He's not worthy of you."

"Is it me?" Old me bubbled, wanting to wallow.

"No." He lifted my chin. "He might not see you, but I do." And then he was kissing me.

I let him, even knowing he did it out of pity. But it deepened from the slanting of his mouth to the thrust of his tongue in my mouth. It drew a moan. The feel of his hands on my hips, drawing me close. Pressing me against him. Making me aware of his erection. For all the kissing I'd done with Darryl, he'd never sported one while holding me.

But Kane did. Kane flirted with me constantly.

Kane was the one to sit me on the hood of the car. It should have been cold, but I'd not felt a chill since I set eyes on him. Not even the icy metal of the hood when he dragged up my skirt. He thumbed me through the fabric, and my breath caught.

I almost came. It had been so long since anyone touched me.

He caught my mouth as he shoved my panties aside. The agony I'd spent over choosing them was unimportant as he fingered me. My head went back as I moaned, bathed in moonlight that tripled as it glinted off snow. I was cold and hot. Coiled tight.

My breath came out in white clouds. My lashes frosted, but I was hot. So very hot and needy. I leaned forward to grab his face and kiss him. His turn to groan and grind, thrusting against me.

I wanted more than that. I reached for him, unbuttoning and unzipping. Gripping him and hearing him suck in a breath. He was thick in my hand. Hard. And then he was inside me.

He slid into me, and I clung to him, my legs around his waist, holding on to his shoulders as he thrust. His fingers dug into my ass cheeks as he pumped. My head went back, and my mouth was open wide, so I saw the fullness of the moon. He kept moving, grinding, harder and harder until I keened, and as I did, I'd have sworn something shot out of the moon.

A stabbing ray of light that entered me. My whole body bowed as I came.

And kept coming. Hard. Blindingly so. I gasped until I remembered to breathe. I shuddered in Kane's arms.

Tingling and spent.

Which was when my date of the night chose to interrupt with a cold, "What's going on?"

19

"DARRYL." HIS NAME SLIPPED FROM MY LIPS IN A hot, embarrassed gasp. I shoved at Kane and scrambled to right my clothes.

Men had it so easy. Kane just had to tuck and zip. Me I had shame tangling my fingers as I tried to yank down my skirt.

"It's almost midnight, and I came looking for you." Darryl pasted a false face on, and for a second, I wondered if I'd misunderstood. Maybe it wasn't him flirting with another while insulting me.

I didn't pussyfoot around it. I bombed him with, "I saw you with that woman."

The change on his face happened subtly. Losing its ah-shucks softness. The corner of his mouth quirked. "What are you talking about? Has Kane been filling your head with lies?"

The more he spoke, the less contrite he sounded.

"He's not the one who's been lying to me," I hotly declared.

"Not sure you can talk, given how I just found you. You were my date, remember? The one you were supposed to fuck at midnight. Guess you couldn't wait that long and went slumming."

The words rudely slapped, and for a moment, stomach-churning shame filled me. Old Naomi would have apologized and groveled. Then stuff my face with anything I could find.

New me? I was filled with wry amusement at the irony. "Drop the offended act. You were playing me the entire time. How dare you act pissed."

"I'll say whatever I like, whore."

He spat the word, and as I stared at him, I wondered, who was this stranger in Darryl's body? Vibrating and angry, in many respects I didn't recognize him. This Darryl frightened me.

Sent a chill into me.

How stupid was I? How could I not have seen the monster inside him? Didn't I learn my lesson with Martin?

"You're drunk, Darryl. Go home." Kane put a hand on my arm, just lightly, and moved so he stood slightly in front of me. The attempt to act protector was appreciated, but unnecessary.

"Not too drunk to kick your ass," Darryl taunted.

"Let's take the testosterone down a notch," I said.

"I'm not talking to you," he snapped. "What I want to know is how drunk Kane is because if I didn't know better, I'd have said Kane actually appeared to be enjoying himself, which I highly doubt is possible. I mean, look at you." Darryl's gaze lasered me. "Hardly a prize."

The insult sucked my breath and hit me hard enough I swayed on my feet

And then I got fucking mad.

I pushed around Kane. "Seriously? What are you, in high school? Stop acting like a self-righteous prick. I have nothing to be ashamed of. I know you were playing me this entire time. Laughing about me with your girlfriend."

"Hardly my girlfriend. More a convenient hole to use when I'm in need."

The crudeness of it brought a moue of distaste. "Go away, Darryl." I'd have his stuff on consignment paid out whether it sold or got insured or not. Cut all ties.

"A prudish whore. Now there's a combination."

"Enough." A soft warning from Kane.

"Or what? What will you do that you haven't already done?"

"Do you really want to know what I'm capable of?" Kane never once raised his voice or moved, yet he'd never appeared more dangerous.

"I think we all know now. So much for your promises."

"I never promised anything, and I would never have gotten involved if you'd managed to keep it together for one more night," Kane growled.

"And you couldn't wait to step in," sneered Darryl.

The thick undercurrent had to do with me, and more than me. The obviousness of their feud slapped me. They hated each other.

I was a pawn. "You've both been using me."

"Took you long enough to figure it out." Darryl snickered.

Whereas Kane remained stony faced. Not one word. No hint of apology.

I hugged myself.

"Don't tell me you actually believed we wanted you," Darryl drawled.

"Why?" I asked. Pathetic, but I couldn't help myself. Did they not realize that their cursed game would hurt me? Did neither of them care?

Kane finally reacted. His lips moved, but Darryl spoke quicker.

"Because you're the guardian of Cambden Lake and the treasure it guards."

"Be quiet," Kane muttered.

"Why? It's too late for her to do anything now. I'm just surprised she hasn't figured it out yet."

Obviously not or I wouldn't cast such a long glance at Kane. I waited for him to say anything. Explain why he'd used me.

Finally, that stony expression cracked a bit. His eyes blazed. "There was no need to be cruel."

"See how he doesn't even try and defend himself," Darryl mocked.

"You fucking idiot," Kane finally growled. "So close to everything and you would ruin it all because you're arrogant."

"I'm arrogant?" Darryl leaned close. "It was never supposed to be you. We agreed. Remember?"

"No, you agreed. Others said nothing." Kane hissed.

I stared on in confusion. "What's going on?" I needed to know. "Kane?" He wouldn't look at me.

"Kane? Explain." I'd seen the duff movies. Please don't let it be the situation where it's see which hot guy beds the ugly woman first.

Darryl kept up his taunting. "I should be

thanking Kane. He did me a favor. We both know you're not exactly in pristine condition. What you'd call ridden hard and put away wet. Tell me, *Kane,* did you pretend it was someone else when you were inside her? It's what I planned to do."

I let out a pained gasp that coincided with the fist that hit Darryl in the mouth. It should have been mine, but I had to admit, Kane's bigger one made a nicer cracking sound.

"Don't you fucking say one more fucking word." Kane bristled, but he came to my defense too late. The damage was already done.

Darryl had used me. Kane had used me. A race to see who would have sex with me first, not because they truly desired me. I stumbled away, and a shiver hit me hard as the cold real world seeped in.

Everyone had been lying. Pretending. I lifted my chin. "You can both fuck off."

"You'll regret betraying me," were Darryl's last words as he left, taking his sneer and disdain with him.

I wanted to shout after him that he wasn't exactly a prize, but I'd not stooped to childish tactics. Not yet, although I reserved the right to change my mind given Kane had yet to flee.

"I'm sorry."

"Bullshit," I spat.

"I'm sorry." He repeated himself, and the asshole actually looked sincere.

"Go away," I snapped at him, holding on to my dignity and tears by a thread.

"Haven't you figured out yet that I can't?"

My laughter was bitter. "I am not falling for your bullshit anymore."

"I might have lied about some things, but my attraction to you is real."

"Stop it. Just stop the lying. Let's both stop faking." I was tired of trying to be confident. Why couldn't it come naturally? Why did the actions of others hit me so hard?

Then again, how had such a magical night gone so horribly wrong?

"That orgasm wasn't fake."

No. And that rattled me because shouldn't sex be more than just about the physical? Then again, how could I claim emotion when until recently I'd harbored a grudge against Kane? "I've seen the women you date." Pictures of the celebrity architect who showed off his creations usually accompanied by someone willowy and elegant.

"Vapid women who can't hope to compare."

"I am not tight and toned like your usual type."

"And? Your body is a testament to your journey."

He made it sound prettier than it was. To me, it appeared more a roadmap of dead ends that showed where you shouldn't go. Two men now had spoken ill of me. Trashed me and my looks. How was I supposed to believe anyone?

Kane tilted my chin to meet his gaze. "What part of 'I find you attractive as you are' do you not grasp?" His hands grabbed my ass, and he yanked me close. Ground me against him. "Do you feel that? Does that feel fake to you?"

The hardness of his erection couldn't be hidden, a stark reminder that, for all the times Darryl kissed me, I'd never noticed a boner.

"Maybe you're just highly sexed," I stated. "Some men can get aroused if the wind blows the right way."

He snorted. "I assure you I have more control than that, except around you. Do you understand how perplexing that is? How frustrating to want the one woman you shouldn't? To crave to the point of ignoring common sense?"

He couldn't be talking about me. It had to be lie. Yet I felt him throbbing against me. I remembered that hardness inside me. Pushing and thrusting.

He'd won the bet with Darryl, so why was he trying to convince me? "What do you want from me?"

"You."

"Liar," I whispered, hating how badly I wanted to forgive him.

"Loving you is probably the one thing I can't lie about." His fingers gripped my head, threaded through my hair, holding me rapt and breathless.

"You don't love me."

"Trust me, I wish I didn't," he muttered before dragging me upwards for a kiss. A deep one, with more French in that moment than I'd learned in all my years of taking it in high school.

Somehow, we ended up in the backseat of his car, the leather warming up as he'd started the engine. Yet that didn't account for all the heat. The chill in me was gone. The moment we touched it was as if passion exploded.

My skirt went up, my panties didn't get pulled aside so much as ripped. I had one foot on the floor of the car, the other bent and in the air, toes almost touching the roof. Kane kissed me, and I felt him pressing against me.

Wanting me again already?

He thrust into me, and I arched under him. He filled me so perfectly, stretching me and touching me in a place that brought a shudder. His lips found mine in a kiss that never ended as he ground into me, pushing his tip against the spot that had me shuddering over and over.

I clung to him and panted into his mouth. Panted his name. "Kane."

He pulled out and slammed in, drawing a sharp cry. Again. I welcomed each slam. Squeezed tight. And this time when I came, I screamed so loud there was no sound. Just me arched in absolute pleasure and his mouth sucking at my shoulder where the flesh lightly throbbed.

He let go of me slowly, as if savoring every last tremor.

I shook from the intensity.

Insane. So public.

I glanced around, wondering if anyone watched. Please don't let me end up with a sex video on the internet.

Twice now, I'd done the wild thing with Kane in the parking lot. What had come over me? Moon madness? A glance to the sky showed the fullness only through a cloudy curtain.

Kane stood outside the car, already tucked away, and there I was splayed like…

I scrambled upright and shoved down my skirt. My panties were gone. My hair a wild mess. Kane held out his hand to me and helped me from the car.

With his cum running down my leg, it occurred to me that we'd not used protection.

I almost fainted.

20

Oh. Shit.

Kane's expression creased. "What's wrong?"

"Condom. We didn't... I'm not... Oh no."

It took him a moment before his expression cleared and he smiled. "One, I'm clean. Two, I'm tied, so no accidental babies."

According to him. What if he was wrong? What if he had super duper sperm? I couldn't become a mom again at my age.

My breath began to frost as a chill moved to beat the heat.

"It's coming," I huffed, the syllables hanging like icicles.

"What is?" he asked.

"The Chill. My enemy." With anyone else that

might have sounded odd, but I knew Kane understood.

He lifted his face to the night air, closing his eyes and tilting his head side to side as if listening, sensing, even tasting. The man I'd had inside my body, and still a stranger in so many respects.

"So that's The Chill. You have nothing to fear," he stated.

"You recognize it?" The words were so cold I could have shattered them. The freezing nature of the air intensified, and I hugged myself, only to have Kane notice and draw me into his body.

"I do, and while frightening, it's harmless to you."

"Doesn't feel harmless. I'm pretty sure it wants to kill me."

"Don't be frightened by it." His fingers wrapped around mine. The Chill receded. "I'll take you home."

"I'm still mad at you." A stupid thing to say since we'd had sex again.

"Then punish me."

"You'd like that," I grumbled.

"If you were the one wielding the whip? Yes. Because it would lead to me worshipping you until you forgive me."

A man shouldn't make me almost come again

with just words. A liar shouldn't be so easily forgiven, and yet I found myself softening. "This is all very confusing to me."

"And I want to explain, but you're tired."

"Not too tired to hear this."

"I will tell you, but I'd rather not do it while trying to drive."

"Afraid I'll hit you?"

"Maybe."

"That bad, eh?" A dry retort.

"Not flattering in some parts, no."

He was being honest, and I admit, I was curious to hear the whole story. And maybe have sex again. As of this moment, I'd turned into one of those confident women portrayed in books and movies, who used men and then discarded them. I'd flipped the script.

"We can talk at my house." I'd hear him out, let him make me come in apology, then kick his ass to the curb, followed by bacon and tequila to console myself, then off to bed where maybe I'd wake up in the morning to a world that made sense.

I settled into the front seat of his car, a sedan with sleek heated leather seats. I relaxed into the comfort of them.

The stereo played a light instrumental number. Kane didn't say much as he drove, one hand on the steering wheel, the other laced with my fingers on the shifter. Remembering what he'd done with that hand, I pressed my thighs together.

Enough already. I needed to distract myself. "It occurs to me your date might be pissed she lost her ride." He'd said he wouldn't be coming alone. And then chose me to go home with.

"No date. I wasn't even planning on going until the last moment."

"Then why tell me you were?"

"Because I wanted to see you jealous."

Not the answer I expected but he'd opened the door to more questions. "What's going on, Kane? Why did you and Darryl make a bet about me?"

"Not a bet. And it involved more than just the two of us."

"More?" I couldn't help but arch a brow and yank my hand free. "Exactly how many people were involved in Operation Seduce the Dumb Divorcee?"

"No one that matters."

His lack of reply angered me. "It matters to me. I have a right to know what twisted game you're playing."

"It's complicated."

"Says you. Or are you agreeing I'm a dumb bitch?" Because I sure as hell felt stupid and could kick myself for getting in the car with him instead of calling for a taxi.

"You are not dumb. You are, however, caught up in events set in motion a long time ago."

"This has to do with my family?" At his nod, I hunkered in my seat. "I don't understand why what my ancestors did has to do with me now."

"Not so much as what they did as what they promised to do. Your family is the key to unlocking—"

A massive moose suddenly appeared in the road in front of us. There wasn't any time to brake. Kane swerved, missing the moose, but slamming into a tree.

I KNEW I WAS IN A DREAM BECAUSE MY GRANDMA was alive.

We were standing by the lake, and I could tell I was young by the pink jelly shoes on my feet. Not the most comfortable things, but everyone had them. Including me, because my father couldn't resist when I begged and batted my lashes.

Grandma was talking about Maddy again and how someday I'd be the one taking care of her because the orcs must never find her.

"Who are the orcs?" Little Me asked even as Old Me wondered.

"They are the enemy, and they must never ever find where the source has been hidden."

"Is the source a treasure?" I asked with all the wide-eyed excitement of a child who'd exulted over pirate stories.

"More like a curse that, if unleashed, will result in the

demise of many. It is up to you, my dear, to keep humanity safe."

"I'll be a good witch," I promised, crossing my heart.

"Hush, little one. Don't let your father hear you say that."

Because Daddy got mad when I talked about magic. So. Mad.

But the weird thing was when Mommy said it, he got sad. Always so sad with my loud Mommy. He never got mad at her until the day she tried to kill me.

As if that were a trigger, I moved from that memory into another one.

I was sitting in a canoe, clutching the sides as my mother paddled us out to the middle of the lake.

The dawning sun provided scant light because of the mist that clung to the surface of the dark water. Spooky, even if Grandma said Maddy wouldn't hurt me. But what if she wasn't the only monster in the lake?

"Where are we going?" I asked, stifling a yawn and huddling in my sweater, tossed over my nightgown.

Mom, finally out of the hospital again, had dragged me out of bed and hurried me out the door. Judging by the mad squawks in the henhouse, Grandma was getting eggs.

She'd stuffed me into the canoe beached on the pebbled shore, no life jacket. Grandma would have been so mad.

And while I'd been cocky about the fact my mother saw me as mature enough to not need one when we set out, in the middle of the lake, I kind of regretted not having it. Especially as my mother stopped rowing and tossed the oars.

"Don't we need those to get back?" I asked, eyeing the far shore.

"We need to be here to stop it."

"Stop what?" I asked.

"The curse. We can end it. Right here, right now."

"I don't understand."

"You don't need to, baby." Mommy cradled my face. "I know what has to be done, and I'll be with you, every step of the way."

With that said, she grabbed hold of me, and dumped us in the cold water!

22

THE SHOCK OF IT ALMOST WOKE ME.

My mother had tried to kill me. Her arms and legs wrapped around me as we sank. I remembered it now.

We sank into a darkness that made the tiny pinprick of light noticeable. How could there be light at the bottom of the lake?

As my lungs tightened, I snapped out of my stupor and struggled. Squirming and kicking at my mother until she released me.

But it didn't stop my descent.

I needed to breathe. I couldn't. I spasmed. My eyes were wide open, watching the light as it brightened, and within it, something moved.

Something came for me. I opened my mouth to scream—

And then I was over the lake, watching as the light rose to the surface. A glow churned the water. From it rose

Maddy, the monster, and atop her snout? The limp form of a child.

Depositing me on the beach, the monster uttered a loud bugle before sliding below the surface. But I saw the beast watching as my father found me and cried out. My ghostly lips wobbled to see him dropping to his kneels to cradle me. Knowing what my mother tried to do, and now having had children of my own, I understood better what drove him. The nightmares that must have plagued him.

Before I could reach out a spirit hand, I was moving again, from the lake to a hospital room. Yet another impossible recollection given that the small shape in the bed, with tubes running out of her, was me. I didn't remember being intubated. Then again, I'd not recalled my mother trying to kill me either.

My father hunched by the bed where he held my hand. Despondent. Broken. Was this where it began, the mood swings that took my happy dad and turned him into a man who alternated between sadness and anger? The doctors had diagnosed him with depression and gave him pills. I could always tell when he'd gone off his meds. The ranting. The crying. The irrationality where I was concerned.

No, you can't leave the house. No. No. No. For a teenager who just wanted to live, I felt stifled.

When he was gone, I'd felt such guilt at the relief. Years later, I now wondered if there was more I could have done.

In the vision, my grandmother entered the hospital,

clutching her bag. Expression fierce, as if ready to do battle.
"Stand aside."

My father didn't look up as he said in a dull monotone,
"This is where it ends."

"Naomi doesn't have to die."

Die?

How could I have forgotten this happened? This couldn't
be real.

My mom had died in a car crash. I was never hospital-
ized other than for a broken arm when I fell off my bike.

*"Maybe it would be better to let her go, knowing what is
to come."* My father cast a bleak gaze at me in the bed.

How could he even think of letting me die?

He glanced at a machine. I'd seen enough medical shows
to know what it measured. Brain waves.

In my case, a flat line. Oh. That wasn't good.

"Is that what you want?" my grandmother asked.

His inner struggle was reflected on his face. In the end,
he bowed his head and whispered, *"Can you fix her?"*

If I'd drowned and lost oxygen to the brain, then no
amount of grandma's soup could fix me.

"Yes."

"If she survives, I am taking her away from here."

Grandma placed a hand on my forehead. *"Running never
works. She'll be back. You know the magic won't give
her up."*

"She deserves a chance at a normal life."

"But she's not normal," was my grandma's reply as she took out a marker and proceeded to draw on me. A healing mark on my forehead, more on my cheeks.

The sigils ignited when Grandma slashed her arm and dripped blood on them. To my surprise, my father roused enough to donate some of his own blood. The body on the bed arched…

Intense pain erupted and drew a sharp cry from me.

"Aah!" I roused to a throbbing agony that radiated in every inch of me. My slitted eyes winced at the bright lights. I could hear a cacophony of noise. Voices. The beeping of machines.

The hysterical voice of my daughter. "Nurse! She's awake! Nu-r-r-s-se!"

If being awake meant suffering, then I welcomed the darkness, returned to the dreams that felt real. Had I recalled pieces of my past?

How had I forgotten?

As if my mind wanted to answer me, I saw myself again as a child at Grandma's house, in the bed with the pink plaid comforter. I didn't sleep peacefully. Nightmares had me thrashing and crying out, "Mommy. No!"

It was my father who rushed in to soothe me, but my grandmother was the one who drew a new symbol and ignited it with a kiss that whispered, "Forget."

And then I was being packed into the car with my dad. I

wore a headset in the backseat, listening to my new Walkman Daddy bought me. Grandma and my father stood outside the car.

"Are you sure you don't want me to help you forget?" she asked.

He shook his head. "She doesn't deserve that despite what she did." He glanced over at me.

"Take care of her."

"I will."

The darkness siphoned me down and spat me out into a room, another hospital, the body in the bed bigger, swaddled head to toe in bandages. Someone was hurt. The tubes emerging from the cocoon hooked into modern machines. Flanking the bed, looking shell-shocked were Geoff and Winnie.

Sad because their Mommy was broken in that bed. I wanted to tell them to not waste their tears, but when I opened my eyes, the pain stole my voice and I sank again. Back into a place where there was no pain. To a place where I was happy before my mother tried to kill me.

Barefoot, and wearing a loose summer dress, I stood on the sandy beach by the lake. A stick in hand, I traced symbols. The same symbols Grandma drew on me after the drowning incident. Circle to circle and around again. Making things whole, then looping them to others to form a chain. The more I traced, the more I could see the logic in how the sigil could be used to heal. A tiny chained set of them covering a whole body could possibly work a miracle.

They could do magic.

In that subconscious place, I drew over and over. Hours. Weeks. Minutes. Eternities.

I kept drawing until my sunny place shadowed. The waves from my tranquil sea turned dark and tossed themselves onto the beach, erasing all my drawings. The rolling tide parted as a figure strode from it.

"Kane?"

He appeared on my beach, tired and disheveled. Gaunt, too. He managed a wan smile. "Hello, sweetheart."

"What's happening?" Because I knew I didn't belong on this beach. Just like I knew Kane wasn't really here.

"You have to wake up, sweetheart."

"I don't want to. It hurts." An understatement. There was a reason why I hid inside my own head.

"I know it hurts, and I wish I could be there to hold you."

"You are here." I stepped toward him, and his shape wavered the moment I reached out. "You're a ghost!"

"In a sense. This place isn't real."

"Am I dead?" I asked.

He opened his mouth and shook his head. "You have to wake up."

"Waking up hurts," I grumbled.

"You can't hide here forever," he said softly. "Can't hide from fate."

"Will you be there?"

"No." And something in the way he said it...

"Kane?"

He looked away from me to the lightning flashing over my lake. "I have to go."

"Go where? Tell me what's going on." I reached for him, but he was gone. I stood alone on my beach, only the numbness I'd enjoyed had gone.

Time to move on and face reality.

Waking up would hurt. Maybe I could minimize it. I dragged my stick in the sand and drew the symbol to heal. Drew it large enough to hold me. I lay within its crook before I dragged a sharp stone over my skin. It hurt and it didn't in this dream place. The blood sure looked red.

I whispered the shape of magic as I leaked into the shape and the spell took hold.

"Heal."

I arched inside the confines of the sigil as power filled it. The power sheeted me. The pain reached a level of ecstasy where I stopped breathing, my heart stilled, and I teetered on the point of death before tumbling back into the land of the living.

23

I WOKE SUDDENLY, MY EYES FLASHING OPEN TO SEE A ceiling made of white tile. The pain I expected didn't materialize. I realized a second too late that I wasn't alone.

"Thank goodness you're awake."

I glanced in incomprehension at the man by my bedside. It took a moment to recognize him.

"Darryl?" He appeared different. Slicker. His hair cut differently, his style of dress more city yuppie than country boy.

"Naomi, you had us so worried." He smiled and said the right things, even grabbed my hands, his grip icy cold against my skin.

I yanked free. "Where am I? What's happening?"

"You were in an accident."

As more clarity returned to me, I realized I wasn't at home but lying in a hospital bed. How had I gotten here? Last I recalled, it was New Year's Eve and...

As I replayed Darryl's betrayal and the events with Kane, I muttered a soft, "Oh."

His ah-shucks look disappeared for a more cunning one. "I see you remember."

"Yup." Every humiliating moment. Where was a nurse when I needed one? I didn't want to deal with Darryl. Not now. Not ever. "Why are you here?"

"To give you a chance to apologize to me."

Maybe it was because I'd just woken up, but his words didn't make sense. "Me apologize? You betrayed me."

"Hardly betrayal since I never made you any promises."

I opened my mouth only to realize that he spoke the truth. He'd never promised I was his one and only. Still... "You pretended to like me."

"And in your desperation, you gobbled it up. Pathetic, really."

I might have been more upset if I hadn't realized something crucial. "You are an asshole. Thank God, I never slept with you."

He frowned, and before he could open his

mouth, I waved my hand. "Now shoo. Begone. I want nothing to do with you." I hoped his skanky girlfriend gave him crabs. Maybe I'd go looking for a spell. Infecto El Crabbio to His Dicki-aye.

"You would have enjoyed it." Darryl suddenly felt a need to reassert his masculinity.

I enjoyed taking it down. "Not likely." I deliberately let my gaze go to his groin and said, "Guess it's possible you're a grower." But my tone said not likely.

"Perhaps it needed more incentive."

"Says you. Could be age related, too. There's a pill for that." As his annoyance grew, I found the strength to sit up, and regretted it. My eyes throbbed.

"You shouldn't insult me given your limited options. With your lover missing, another needs to step in and take his place."

"What?" I tried to comprehend once more what he was saying, wishing the pounding behind my eyes would abate. And why was it so hot? Every single pore of my body oozed sweat. I could feel it soaking my thin hospital nightgown, drenching my hair. A lovely time for a hot flash.

Darryl took on a sneer as he said, "Let me say this slowly so you understand. The one you know as Kane is gone."

"Kane is gone?" It took me a second to put the pieces together. "He was in the car with me."

"They say it's a miracle you're alive. Apparently, someone didn't want you to be the one when the time came."

"No one tried to kill me. It was an accident." The moose came out of nowhere.

"Impressive the number of times you've eluded death. But in the end, you'll still die."

"Is that a threat?"

"A promise. Even you can no longer derail a plan put into play centuries ago."

"I won't let you kill me," I stated.

"You won't have a choice. Especially now that your cheating lover is out of the way."

"Kane's not dead." After all, I'd survived. Surely, he had, too.

"Then where is he?" Darryl asked. "Because no one's seen him since that night. Just the wreck of his car and your broken body. I tell you lots of folks were hoping you'd die and leave the legacy to one of your progeny. Problem being, there's no time to properly wake the guardian magic in them."

"You're not making any sense. I want you to leave." Hard to sound forceful when you're dizzy in bed, soaking the sheets, and pretty sure you smell like a locker room full of hockey players just coming off the ice and a hard practice.

"I'll go but think upon my words. When the time comes, we can do this the easy way, or the hard." Darryl left, and I heaved out a breath.

What the hell was that about? And could it be true? Had Kane died in the crash?

I lay there, shell shocked and sweaty, which was how Winnie found me.

"Mom. You're awake!" She threw herself at me for a hug. It took me a second to squeeze her back. "Figures you'd regain consciousness when I go for a pee."

"I thought peeing was an old lady thing," was my weak croak.

Winnie pulled away and offered a wan smile. "You're not old. How do you feel?"

I felt...remarkably better than expected. "I'm okay. I think. What happened? How long was I out?" I didn't ask the most burning question yet: Where was Kane?

"You've been unconscious since New Year's Day. The accident happened after midnight sometime."

"How long have I been unconscious?" I expected to hear hours, maybe days.

"Almost a month."

My jaw hit the floor, crawled away, and left me unable to speak.

Winnie hastened to explain. "You were hurt really bad when the car hit that tree."

"Because of the moose. It came out of nowhere," I whispered. "It was huge."

"So was the tree." Winnie's laughter was shrill. "It didn't help that, for some reason, the air bags didn't deploy and your seatbelt snapped. You shot out the windshield and hit the ground over twenty feet away."

I had a vague recollection of Kane yelling and flinging out his hand. Saving me?

"How badly was I hurt?"

Winnie glanced away. "Bad. The doctors didn't think you'd survive."

I clutched at the sheet and shifted. Where was the pain? Shouldn't there be pain? "What kind of injuries did I have?" Obviously not that severe given I'd healed in a month.

"So this is the weird thing. You had just about every bone broken. You were in a cast, Mom. Neck to toe. They said you'd never walk again your spine was so messed up."

"Impossible." I glanced down at my body hidden by the bedding. I wiggled my feet and legs. Saw them moving. "I feel fine." A bit sluggish and lightheaded, but otherwise fine.

"No kidding, impossible. The doctors are calling you a medical miracle."

It was then I understood what had happened. "You used a magical sigil to heal me."

"Not me. And not for lack of trying. You'd think Grandma's book of spells would have something about healing. Even my online sources didn't have anything that could do more than ease a fever or help hair grow."

"The healing sigil is easy. It looks like this." I went to trace it on the sheet covering my lap, only to pause. My finger hovered as the shaped dangled out of my reach. "I can't remember," I muttered.

"Are you saying you healed yourself?" Winnie squeaked. "Since when can you do magic? I thought you didn't believe."

"Hard to ignore it when it tries to kill you."

Rather than look shocked, Winnie nodded. "I heard about some of the attempts, but Jace says most of them stopped once you fully activated the house defenses."

"Exactly how much does Jace know?" And why hadn't he told me? He'd certainly done his damnedest to convince me to leave. Why not give me the real reason why?

"He knows more than he's telling, that's for

sure." Winnie grimaced. "And trust me, I've been trying to loosen his tongue." I really didn't want to know how she attempted that.

"You're still together?" I asked.

"And going strong. What can I say? I like my men mature."

"Be careful." I couldn't help the mommy moment.

"I will, Mom. I'm not expecting marriage and kids, if that's what you're worrying about. It's more that he's hot, excellent in bed, plus he knows stuff about this lake."

"Good luck getting him to talk. Kane never would." I said his name and waited. Waited for her to tell me he was in a bed down the hall.

Winnie's gaze dropped, and she clasped and unclasped her hands. "About Kane."

My stomach turned into a marble-sized ball. "He's dead, isn't he?"

"That's the belief."

"What's that supposed to mean? Didn't they find his body?"

"The car burned."

"And? Remains don't evaporate. There would have been bones."

She shook her head.

"Then he must have been ejected from the car like me."

"They searched the forest and the road."

"He can't be gone." I'd yet to explore my feelings for him. To truly ponder if he was real and honest when he said he saw my flaws as marks of pride. I hadn't decided if I would forgive him for using me. I definitely wanted more sex with him. More of the passion that brought me to life.

"I'm sorry," Winnie said. "I didn't even know you were friends with him."

Now wasn't the time to explain how we'd become more in that last moment. It surprised me she didn't ask about Darryl. A man I'd misjudged. A guy who had used me. I just couldn't see to what purpose. "Darryl was here."

"What the hell did that twat waffle want?"

"He came to tell me Kane was dead." I didn't repeat the other crazy stuff.

"What a douchebag."

It seemed as good a time as ever to say, "I dumped Darryl at that party."

"I know. I called him to let him know you were in the hospital, and he had the nerve to ask me out!"

"Turns out he wasn't who I thought."

My daughter grabbed my hand. "Happens to the best of us."

Winnie didn't get to stay long because once the nurses realized I was awake, they came flying in on rubber-soled shoes and smock tops to flock me.

I was their miracle patient, and it wasn't long before I wanted to escape their clutches. They, however, insisted on running a battery of tests. I let them take some blood and my blood pressure, even my temperature, but I drew the line at anything else until I had a shower.

Once I was naked I got the most shocking surprise of all. I blinked and rubbed my eyes. Then I rubbed myself like I was an oil lamp with a genie inside.

Not only did I not have a single broken bone or bruise, my healing had gone deeper.

I'd given myself a makeover. A magical tummy tuck and boob job along with a replenishing boost to my skin that had dealt with the dry skin.

I groped myself. Squeezed my boobs. They were mine. I palmed my flat tummy.

Flat.

Fuck.

Seriously. Fuck.

The cellulite on my thighs? Gone.

Surreal. I kept patting my body in the hospital

bathroom, feeling the flesh and coming to grips with the fact it was mine, if slightly modified. I think I would have been freaked out more if I'd not noticed the imperfections left behind. The spell had not turned back the arms of time. The silvery lines, marking my pregnancies, remained as grooves in my skin. The crow's feet by my eyes—with the thicker lashes—gave me character. I looked like a woman in her forties who'd taken care of herself.

With the most awesome flat belly. I couldn't stop staring down, noticing the bush. Lush and thick. Wait a second. I could see it. No sagging flesh in the way.

Could a spell have done all this? Or could it be that autophagy, a process where body would process excess skin and fat to survive, was the root cause? After all, I'd been asleep for a month.

It made me wonder, was I on a machine that whole time? How did they feed me? So many questions about what happened while I slept.

But the biggest one of all?

Had I healed myself inside my mind? It seemed farfetched, but then again, what I knew of magic wouldn't even fill a tiny cup.

The only person who might know was gone.

What had happened to me? Why couldn't I remember the symbol? If I could heal...I could...

I frowned. Healing the world would kill me. So how would I pick and choose? What if I saved a bad person? What if I didn't save the good?

How could I decide?

Despite the doctors wanting to run even more tests on me to see if they could decipher my miracle of healing, I fled. For one, the food totally sucked. A person could only eat so much sugar free Jell-O. Two, I'd already had six people sneak in to ask me to heal a friend or relative. And three, I was pretty sure one of my nurses was possessed. By a good-looking ghost, but still, possessed. I saw it shimmering inside her, not always fitting within her body.

Want to bet if I mentioned it, the doctors would keep me and analyze me a little further?

No thanks. I checked myself out under the supervision of my kids, who tucked me into the front seat of Winnie's car. Geoff rode in the back, his hand on my shoulder for support.

The reminder I wasn't alone helped quite a bit. Lying in that hospital bed, I'd felt confined. Strangers all around me, too cheerful, too talkative.

I just wanted to go home and be surrounded by my things. I wanted to see my cat. My bed. Pajamas where my ass didn't hang out.

As we pulled into the drive, the house welcomed

me. Not in words or acts, just a general sense of wellbeing. Relief.

It felt good to be home.

Geoff bounced ahead to open the door.

Excited, I called out to my pet. "Grisou. I'm home. Where are you baby?" I hoped he wasn't disappointed I didn't arrive with any treats. Usually when I called him, I had something from the butcher that I knew he'd like.

I saw the shadow of a massive cat come bounding before the beast itself popped into view. Bigger than a lion with my Grisou's face.

What the hell?

And that wasn't the weirdest part. His meow—which boomed enough to make me blink—was followed by an indignant, "Where have you been? You know I hate sleeping by myself."

24

Geoff hauled my ass up off the floor. "Mom, are you okay?"

No, I was not okay. My cat was the size of a pony. And he spoke. Maybe I should have stayed in the hospital.

"Grisou startled me," I admitted, looking down and getting a confusing dual view. In one, my normal-sized cat twined between my legs purring. In the imprint over it, ginormous kitty was practically knocking me over. Also purring. Not as soft and cute when multiplied in size.

I had to be hallucinating.

"I think you should go lie down," a worried Winnie suggested.

"Good plan." A good night's sleep in my bed would do just the trick.

The wide stairs came in useful as my son insisted on supporting me up, not trusting me to walk. I could understand the concern. I'd been flat on my back and unmoving for a month. Geoff probably assumed adrenaline kept me upright. I should have told him I felt too good to crash. Like, seriously awesome. I didn't even remember the last time I'd felt this great.

Geoff brought me right to the edge of my bed, followed by Winnie, who hovered.

"I'm fine." I tried to get rid of them.

"Let me get your shoes." She dropped to her knees, and I waved her off.

"I can take them off myself. Go. Shoo. I'll be fine."

They protested.

Cute kids. But would they leave already?

In the safety of my room I wanted a peek at my nude body in a better mirror and light.

Selfish?

Yup.

I'd not looked this fit in more than twenty years. I wanted to enjoy it.

I stripped my ass naked and got a full-length look in my new tall mirror. I stared for a long while at the body I'd been hoping to eventually get. I'd entertained this dream that the store would do well enough that I could hire Winnie. Maybe even have enough to book myself in for a mommy makeover.

Plastic surgery to fix the things diet couldn't. I'd done my research. Seen the pics and read all the threads. I'd known what to expect. The discomfort. The sleeping in a recliner for weeks as the stitches healed. The drains I'd have to monitor, easing fluid from my body. Why would anyone agree to be sliced and diced?

Unless you'd had to lift your tummy to wash under or had breasts that literally hung like tube socks it was hard to understand why anyone would do it. But I'd hated my body for so long that while I winced at the mastopexy procedure—mine would require an anchor cut that would remove excess skin and reattach the nipple (Can anyone say zombie nipple?)—the end result would be a firm boob that pointed forward.

Exactly what I saw in the mirror, done with magic and saving myself weeks of grief.

Cool. Along with my improvements, I saw the marks of my journey.

My appendix scar? Still a white slash on my side. My tummy, thighs, and breasts bore stretch marks. The hair down below curled a steely and dark gray. Say hello to the me I would have been if I'd not used food as a crutch.

Grisou parked his furry butt beside me, the big version.

Oddly enough, I didn't fear him. That was my cat. Even if he was mega sized.

"Have you always been this big?" I asked, reaching over to ruffle the fur on top of his head.

Only to see in the mirror that my hand stretched oddly down to the short version being reflected. I stared at the glass then my cat. Then the mirror again as I held my hand above Grisou's giant head and saw it reflected in a way that made me wince.

"I take it the secret is out."

"Argh." Yeah. That was my mature reply to my cat talking to me.

His giant eyes didn't blink. He stared until I fidgeted.

"Are you going to eat me?" Asked every human before a massive set of jaws unhinged.

"Depends. Did you smuggle out any bodies? Or bring back the loose skin bits you lost?" My cat was definitely talking.

A part of me thought I should scream. But I was Naomi, who'd seen and used magic, faced down demons and The Chill. Was I really going to get freaked out that my pet could communicate?

"Since when can you talk to me?"

"Since the day we met. Not my fault you're hard of hearing." He licked a paw and slicked his fur back.

"How come I can hear you now?"

"Because you're finally turning into the witch you were meant to be."

"Making you my familiar."

My cat hissed. "Implying I'm your slave. Not likely, witch." That quickly, he went hostile.

Definitely my pet. How many times had I been petting him and he purred, only to suddenly attack? "If you're not my familiar, then what are you?"

"None of your business." Said with a haughty air.

"And here I thought we were best friends."

"A best friend wouldn't try and keep me locked up in the house." Giant pussy pouted.

I snorted. "Since when has a door stopped you from getting outside?"

"The house isn't always cooperative with my excursions."

Interesting the cat spoke of the house as sentient. "Do you talk to the house?"

"Do you talk to the vacuum?" was his sassy reply.

"I used to talk to the robot one we had at my

old house." I wanted to be known as the polite human if Skynet ever did come to pass.

"That's weird."

"So is a talking cat."

"Am I talking, or are you going crazy?" he purred.

I blinked, and I swear he smirked.

"No, I am not crazy," I huffed.

"If we ignore the fact you're talking to your pet."

"Everyone talks to their pets," I argued.

"How many of them reply?" He looked so damned smug, until he suddenly dove at his hindquarters for a fierce lick.

"You can't be the only talking cat in the world."

"Only special people can hear me."

"Like who? Who else do you talk to?"

"Trish, and a few others. But soon many more will be able to hear my voice."

"Speaking of Trish, I should call her. Let her know I'm home." My best friend must have been so worried. So worried, she never came to see me in the hospital. Or maybe she had but I didn't know because of the whole coma thing. Had to be.

I exited the bathroom naked and glancing constantly at my boobs. I poked a nipple for fun and watched it retract. It worked. Yay. I'd read stories about franken nubs, filed under the boob jobs gone wrong.

I skimmed a hand over my flat tummy. Flat. Damn. I couldn't help but palm it.

Check me out. Darryl thought I'd come crawling back? Ha. Not with this body I wouldn't.

I could see why women loved doing revenge videos. The next time he saw me, I totally wanted to make him regret his behavior and cruel words.

Knowing what I did now, I wished I'd given Kane a chance. He'd always seen me as desirable. If only he weren't dead.

He's not.

The certainty filled me. False hope, given what everyone said. But I clung to it. So long as there was no body, I could believe he lived. Lost in the woods. He'd return or be found. We'd make up and have sex. Lots of sex.

Naked-with-the-lights-on kind of sex.

I dressed in pajamas and glanced around for reading material. Nothing. Not even Grandma's old books. Should I pop downstairs to grab something? Winnie told me to go to bed. Only I wasn't tired. She'd give me heck if she saw me gallivanting around. She and Geoff were like clucking hens.

Gawd, I loved my kids. Nice to know they appeared to reciprocate.

I hesitated by the stairs. I was being a ninny. I had every right to go downstairs and get a book if I wanted to. It was my house.

I still snuck, slowing as I heard voices coming from the kitchen. Winnie and the deeper timbre of Jace.

"Pack your things. Come home with me, tonight."

"You know I can't leave her." My kid still thinking I needed babysitting.

"Staying here with her will only make it harder in the long run," he advised.

"She's my mother."

"A shitty mother, according to you."

Wait, what? The blow of it hurt.

"It wasn't all her fault. That bastard Martin didn't help the situation."

Since when did Winnie call her dad Martin? It hit me in a cold slap. She'd read the book. Oh God. I sat on the top step, trying to not be sick.

"You can't soften now. You know there's no other real choice."

"Yeah, I know." I heard the rustle of fabric. I closed my eyes but still imagined her hugging Jace.

I wanted to rush down and confront them. Wanted to beg my daughter's forgiveness and, at the same time, let her understand she didn't have to stick around out of duty. Old me would have snuck back upstairs. New Naomi loudly thumped each step as I headed for the main floor.

By the time I could see the kitchen, Winnie stood by herself by the kitchen island. My daughter offered me a wan smile. "Mom, what are you doing out of bed?"

"I heard voices. What's up?"

"Nothing." My daughter lied.

My lips pinched. "Didn't sound like nothing."

"Jace came over."

"And?"

My daughter fidgeted. "Just discussing the fact that once you're all better, maybe I should start looking for a new place."

"You want to move out? I thought things were better between us."

"They are, but—"

I interrupted. "Whatever it is, I can fix it. Please." Desperate, yet it still came out of my mouth.

Her expression froze. "It's not you, Mom. It's… Ah… Jace asked me to move in with him."

"Oh." I pasted a bright smile on my face. "Guess things are going great then."

"Awesome," my daughter said woodenly. "Never better."

"You don't sound convinced," I pointed out.

"I don't think I should be leaving you right now, after everything you've been through."

The reminder of my loss tightened my throat. "I'm fine. Never better, so don't worry about me. Just came down for a drink." I grabbed a water bottle from the fridge and waved it. "I think I'm going to lie down." I treaded heavily up the stairs before quietly sneaking back down a few steps so I could listen.

Sure enough, Jace returned. "Are you okay?" he asked.

"That was awkward," my daughter muttered.

"Only because you feel guilt. It's normal."

Guilt about what? Because she'd hidden her relationship with Jace, or something else?

"I wish I didn't have to keep it a secret," Winnie lowly stated. "She deserves to know."

To know what? Was there a bigger secret than her wanting to shack up with my neighbor?

"How will knowing the date of her death help?"

Death? What were they talking about? I almost marched down there to demand answers, but given they'd already blown me off once, I listened.

"I know telling her won't help, but how can I keep pretending everything is okay when it's not?"

"You can't say anything." Jace sounded quite

firm. "What if she begs you to save her? What if she asks you to take her place?"

"She wouldn't," Winnie said softly.

"Do you really think your mother would sacrifice herself for you?"

The dead silence hurt most of all because I knew I'd do anything for my kids.

I crept up the stairs with those words ringing in my head.

What were Jace and Winnie talking about? Why did they both speak as if my death were a foregone matter?

Unless…maybe I didn't fully heal from the accident. Maybe something inside me was broken. Unfixable.

Could Winnie be trying to spare me the news of a fatal cancer or other ticking time bomb?

Or was this related to the secret everyone tiptoed around?

It was enough to make me scream. But instead, after a good night's sleep, I decided to go looking for answers.

25

I BOUNCED DOWN THE STAIRS THE NEXT DAY, startling Winnie and Geoff, who both froze and eyed me as if guilty of conspiracy. Which they were. Something obviously ailed me, and they both knew about it. I could have been annoyed by their silence, or I could see it for the gesture it implied. A deep, abiding affection for me.

I appreciated it. I was their mother. They loved me, and I loved them. I'd give my life for them, but that didn't mean I wasn't curious.

"What's wrong?"

"Nothing." Geoff answered too quickly, turning to the stove and flipping bacon.

"How you feeling?" Winnie asked.

"Great for a dying woman."

Her face blanched. Geoff's shoulders tensed.

"What are you talking about?" Winnie whispered.

"You can stop pretending. I know something is wrong with me. Is it cancer?"

The relief on Winnie's face was almost comical. "You don't have cancer."

"I heard you and Jace saying I was doing to die." I admitted to my spying.

Winnie's relief turned to caution. "You must have misunderstood."

"Did I? Because you both sounded pretty certain about it."

"You're being ridiculous, Mom. Don't you think if you were dying, we'd do something to stop it?"

Lie. Lie. Lie.

"Geoff, care to say something?" Because he'd remained cooking with his back to me.

"Actually, yeah, I do have something to say." He whirled and presented a still sizzling slice of bacon on his spatula. "Breakfast?"

As if I'd say no. But I wasn't done harassing my kids. "So if I'm not dying of cancer, what's really going on? Does this have to do with the lake? Our family?"

Geoff opened his mouth as if to speak, but Winnie shook her head.

"I have a right to know," I stated.

"Don't talk to me about rights. I read Martin's diaries."

Ouch. "You shouldn't have." How I wished I'd burned them. Even dead, that bloody man was fucking shit up.

"I disagree. They were enlightening."

"Winnie, about what you read—"

She cut me off. "I have to go." She fled, and I let her go. How could I tell her I didn't remember cheating on Martin? Didn't know who might have fathered her?

Troubled, I had another piece of bacon and eyed my son. "I take it you read them, too."

"Enough to wish I wasn't related to this family." And then he stalked off.

Everything always came back to my family and the secrets.

Grabbing a coffee, and more bacon, I fled to my room, munching the ambrosia of the gods. Crunchy. Salty. Yum. It didn't cure my agitation.

Despite knowing they were gone, I peeked under the bed. Martin's box was gone. But so were my grandmother's books.

"Where are they?" I muttered as I paced my room, eyeing the shelves, peeking in the wardrobe and my drawers.

My cat, who took up a large portion of my bed,

kept his eyes closed as he said, "The female child took the books."

"All of them?"

The yawn my cat enjoyed provided an answer.

"Why did she take them?" Asked aloud even as I recalled the pages sliced out of the recipe book. What was in there that Winnie didn't want me to see?

I wished I had someone to talk to.

Trish had yet to answer any of my texts. Marjorie's phone remained silent, too. Had something happened to them?

"Do you know what's going on?" I asked my cat. Not the first time, I should add.

"A lack of quiet," was his complaint.

"Why can't I ever get a straight answer?"

"People tried and you called them crazy. Refused for the longest time to believe. You reap what you sow."

"Not helpful," I grumbled. "I believe now."

"Only because you were slapped by the evidence."

"Evidence of what? Magic? Fine. But what about the rest? Why all the danger? The drama? Why does it feel as if I'm missing something important?"

My cat didn't reply but tucked his head into his body.

"How can you sleep at a time like this?"

"By closing my eyes."

"I can't stay here all day. I need to get out."

"Go where?" my cat demanded.

"As if I need to tell you." Then again, Grisou did ask. "I thought I'd go into the shop, see what still needs to be done before reopening."

"Not much point given it was condemned by the town."

According to my knowledgeable feline, it was deemed unsafe after the fire. There went my plans to reopen anytime soon. The world appeared ready to knock me down, but I wasn't going down without a fight. I'd find the money to rebuild.

I refused to stay in the house. I wandered down to the beach and the frozen lake. I don't know what I expected to find. Maddy was dead.

Mom, Dad, Grandma, too.

My friends weren't answering. My kids were hoarding secrets and had disappeared on me. And to top it off, Kane was missing.

I couldn't just sit around waiting for answers. Time to go find some. I enlisted the aid of my lazy feline, because he was the only one I could trust right now, and besides, weren't cats keen trackers?

"Grisou! I need your help."

"I'm napping," he reminded me as I did my best to tug his giant carcass off the bed.

"This is important."

"So is my sleep," he grumbled.

"I'll stop by the butcher for some fresh fish."

"How many kilos?"

"As many as it takes to get you in my car." Which protested the moment he sat in the back. It had me asking, "How is it I never saw any of the clues before? I mean, the ass end of the car is sitting lower by at least a few inches."

"Did you just call me fat?" His face wedged between the seats.

"No. I want to understand how you can fake being small."

He smiled. Too many teeth in it. "Magic. Now drive, chauffeur witch. And not too fast so I can enjoy the scenery."

"Have you always been this demanding?" Only to answer myself. "Yes, yes you have." My own fault. I'd spoiled him as a kitten.

The crash site proved harder to find than expected. I drove by it twice before Grisou snapped, "Would you stop going back and forth? It's right there. How blind are you?"

Apparently plenty because I never imagined the

humped snow windrowed on the shoulder hid the site of an accident. One month of winter weather had concealed the marks of the crash.

The sharp winter air filled my lungs as I exited the car. It didn't have the freezing terror of the Chill, just a cleansing cold.

Grisou stalked alongside me, stopping by a massive tree, the bark mangled. I brushed the snow away, revealing the damage and the clinging specks of paint. Had this been an accident?

Could someone have made us see something that wasn't there? But why? Was it about getting rid of me or Kane? I had to wonder because no one ever finished the job in the hospital.

My cat stalked into the forest and only stopped long enough to mutter, "Are you coming or not? You know I could be at home sleeping by the woodstove."

"Yes, your majesty," I muttered.

"That's more like it, although I prefer 'your eminence,' accompanied by a freshly opened case of tuna."

"Would you like me to address you as your high-ness, too?"

"You do realize the favor I do you by allowing you to serve me."

Every single meme I'd read about cats. True. So very, very true.

My cat moved farther into the woods than I liked before stopping. "This is where his trail ends."

"Whose trail?"

"The other person in the car."

"Wait, you mean we've been tracking Kane this entire time?"

"I've been tracking. You're merely stumbling after me."

"Keep up that attitude and it will be dry diet kibble, you oversized furball."

"I heard that."

"Good. I want to know how you can follow anything. It's been a month. It's snowed and stuff. Surely there's nothing to track." Just because a Flintstone-sized cat talked to me didn't mean I'd take its words as gospel.

"I'm lying. Let's go home." His tail lifted, and he was ready to march off, only I didn't follow.

I glanced around then up. In the movies shit always dangled from branches. Nothing popped out, but I noticed something interesting. Lots of broken twigs and branches. I glanced around at the trunks and saw one was splintered.

"There was a fight here." The more I looked, the more I could see a series of different colored auras. Only one of the streamers flowed almost black. It meandered alongside the tracks I'd left. Looking behind, I noticed a sizzling silver thread ran out of me in an ethereal filament.

I blinked and waved my hand at it. The thread remained. "What do you call that?"

"The stuff I follow."

"Essence of people?" I ventured.

"You could just stick with time-honored scent."

"This is more than smell, though." I reached to touch a thread, and my hand went through it, making it ragged and wispy.

"What happened?" I asked.

"You're messing it up, like those who took him."

Rather than ask what he meant, I looked around again, this time unravelling the threads from each other. The dark thread didn't leave the clearing.

"If a scent disappears, does that mean the person is dead?"

"Not always. He lives."

"So where did Kane go?"

"No idea. His trail just stops."

"That doesn't help me." Frustration built in me.

"What are you going to do then?" my cat taunted.

"I want him back!" I clenched my fists. I wanted

something to go right for once. I wanted to feel as if I were in control.

A mist appeared amongst the tree trunks.

Grisou's hackles rose, and he rumbled, "Danger."

"No duh." The syllables frosted, but I wasn't about to run. This was the first time I'd encountered The Chill in the daytime. Had it expanded its abilities? Would I finally meet the threat?

"Who are you?" I shouted. "Show yourself!" The words dropped like icicles that shattered in the silence.

The tendrils of cold whispered, but I couldn't understand. I did feel a longing. To let go. To allow The Chill to invade me.

Surrender.

Never.

I knelt on the ground even as my cat protested, "What are you doing?"

"Magic." I hoped. Only I had no canvas to write. The snow around me was crunchy in spots. I couldn't draw.

I needed a better surface. Like the road. I'd better move fast, though. The fog was thick enough that someone, or something, could have been standing only a few feet from me and I wouldn't see them.

"We need to get to the car."

"Run," was my cat's advice as he led the way through the woods back to the car.

I followed, feet crunching snow, the icy fog thickening and swirling around me. Piercing my lungs. Making me breathe even harder.

The whispers grew louder, as if to overcome the panting from my taxed lungs. Oddly enough, it wasn't fear animating me the most but adrenaline. I wanted something to fight.

Reaching the car, I grabbed the handle of the door. My mitten stuck to the metal. Froze to it. I yanked, clicking the mechanism, and slid my hand free as the door opened. Grisou's fat furry butt bolted inside first. The engine that I'd left running chugged sluggishly, and the lights dimmed as the fog began to spill from the forest onto the shoulder of the road.

"Do something," my cat demanded.

"I'm trying." I reached in and grabbed the chalk I'd stashed in the plastic bucket molded into the console.

I knelt on the black asphalt, mostly gray with salt this time of the year. My chalk had no problem scraping a line. Up. Over. I drew the light symbol, one big enough to keep The Chill at bay. I blew on it, and the warmth encased me in a bubble.

Still, The Chill pressed on me.

It wanted something.

Well, I wanted something back.

Without even thinking about it, I drew again on the road, a symbol of query. What are you? A spell of identity that resulted in the mark turning opaque.

Swirling with color and smoke.

What. Are. You.

I scraped my finger, tracing the lines and willed it with my intent.

Perhaps that was why when the image cleared, I saw myself.

26

IT SPOOKED ME. ESPECIALLY SINCE THE MOMENT I saw myself The Chill disappeared. Left as if it were never there.

"If you're done doodling, I'm hungry. Let's go get my food," my cat complained.

Before I got in the car, I cast a last glance around. I don't know what I expected to see. The world appeared as it should, a woody, wintery wonderland. Yet underneath that cold, I'd have sworn I felt the land trembling. A sense of anticipation clung to the air that only increased as I returned to town.

The butcher had plenty of deals for me, and I placed them in the trunk despite my cat protesting from the front seat.

As I headed down the last road to my cottage, I drove on semi-automatic, paying enough attention to make it safely while pondering the deepening mystery all around me. The many pieces and clues refused to cooperate. How did everything tie together? I couldn't ignore the ominous undercurrent surrounding me, especially since I'd woken up. And didn't just mean from my coma.

I needed to figure out what was happening. And that included finding Kane. Grisou claimed he was alive. At least he'd left the clearing that way, but he'd been taken by people who knew how to obscure their tracks.

Maybe they'd not hidden him too far.

I thought of telling Winnie so she could mention it to Jace. After all, he and Kane were related. However, by the time I got home, I vetoed that idea. What if I marched over to Jace's house and she was there, doing stuff with him. I'd rather be an ostrich with my head in the sand than have that picture in my head.

Once home, a hot tea in hand, I nestled in my chair with a book, and nothing else. Perhaps if I let my mind relax, everything would finally make sense.

I didn't enjoy it for long. There was a brisk

knock on the door, which I debated ignoring. Call it a gut feeling. I doubt I wanted to see who stood on the other side.

Ding. Ding.

Since when did I have a doorbell?

"Mom, why aren't you answering?" my son complained, appearing from the basement and trotting to the door. He swung it open and grimaced. "Officer Murphy."

"Mr. Dunrobin. I'm here to see your mother."

"She's resting."

"It's important I speak to her."

"Says you." Geoff stepped outside with Murphy and shut the door.

Seriously? I wasn't a child to be sheltered from things. About to swing my legs off the chair, the door suddenly opened, and Geoff came stamping in, hugging himself. "It is cold outside. I'm going to make some coffee."

Murphy hovered in the doorway.

I wondered if I could subtly signal Geoff to throw a little something in my drink. By the expression on Murphy's face, and Geoff's too-bright attitude, I didn't think I'd like what came next.

Murphy towered in the entrance, sporting a giant mustache, lush sideburns, and a cowboy hat.

I'll admit, while it initially threw me, I'd come to enjoy the look.

He removed his hat. "Ms. Rousseau—"

"Get inside," I said with a wave of my hand. "You're letting out the heat." Once a mom paying bills, always a mom paying bills. Not to mention, it was better for the environment.

Murphy shut the door and eyed his boots before kicking them off to enter farther. "Sorry to disturb you. I see you're resting."

"I take it you're here to talk to me about the accident." His office probably needed some kind of report. I was just surprised it didn't happen in the hospital.

"I am. There's been a development in the missing person's case of Kane D'Argent."

"You found him!" My tone emerged bright and hopeful.

His expression appeared anything but. "We did."

Within minutes, I'd politely thanked Murphy and then left him with my son so I could go lie down.

Lie down being code for crying my face off. Apparently, they found his body. It wasn't burned up in the crash as they'd initially thought. It wasn't pretty given he'd been injured by the fire then dragged off by wild animals. They were waiting on dental records, but given his wallet was located nearby...

Kane was declared officially dead.

My gut said that was wrong. I wanted to deny it, but at one point, how could I deny the evidence? As the truth set in, I cried.

Oh, how I cried.

Not my best look. I'm an ugly crier. Blotchy face. Snot. Eyes of an addict, bloodshot and weepy. No amount of cold water could remove all the puffiness and damage. Sleep would, but I needed something to drink. I'd dehydrated myself with that epic cry.

I might cry again. Better fill up the snot tank.

A peek down the stairs showed no one around. Good. I wasn't ready to talk to anyone, so of course, a knock made me jump ten feet in the air. Like I literally almost slammed my head.

Then I hugged myself. The last knock brought the shittiest news. Was I really going to answer?

Where was someone when I needed them? Grisou didn't appear to be around. The kitchen only had the light over the stove shining. Geoff was downstairs for the night.

Nothing good ever happened answering a door after dark.

Knock. Knock. Brisk, no nonsense. Would they go away?

I prodded my house. *Friend or foe?*

No reply, and still no cat, just me.

I have nothing to fear. It was just answering a door. Maybe a few words spoken.

I stalked over and flung it open to see a beautiful young woman wearing a brand-new baby blue parka that set off the very red hair cascading in playful waves. Brilliant green eyes perused me.

The beautiful woman smiled, and her words held a hint of accent as she said, "You must be Ms. Rousseaux."

"I'm sorry. Who are you?" I felt like I should know who she was, only the hair was wrong. Shouldn't it be a silver bob and brown eyes? My eyes widened as I recognized who it was.

"Helena?" Geoff's timing couldn't have been better—or maybe worse. He emerged from the basement, and I had little time to recover.

"Of course, you're Helena. I don't know how I didn't recognize you." I felt all kinds of dumb since I'd seen a picture of her. Geoff sent it to me as part of their engagement announcement. I'd found out with everyone else. Was I a little bitter Trish was told personally? My own fault for not having a better relationship with Geoff. Trish would have probably recognized Helena and not appeared like an ass.

"Not your fault, Mom. Helena's a pro at changing her look." He reached for his fiancée's hands and squeezed them. "What are you doing here?"

"I came to see you of course." She simpered up at him.

Was it wrong I disliked her instantly?

"I thought we'd agreed on some time apart."

"No, you asked for it. I gave, and now I'm here to say I'm sorry."

Was I the only one who wanted to gag? Surely Geoff didn't buy her overdone apology.

"You flew all this way? But what about your job?"

"You're more important."

Gag me with a spoon.

I saw my son wavering. So did the barracuda at my door. I saw her other shape waver into view. Not as pretty or frail looking as the body she'd possessed.

"Don't let her in," I exclaimed.

"Mom. What the hell?"

Don't say it. Don't say it. "She's a demon." I couldn't help but blurt it aloud.

My son gaped. "Mom. What is wrong with you?"

"I'm sorry. I shouldn't have come." Helena gave a fake sniffle, but the thing inside her smirked.

"Don't be ridiculous. Come inside." Geoff invited her in, and the house did nothing to stop it. Did that mean she wasn't dangerous? Or had the accident broken my link to it?

Helena offered a simpering smile at my son. "Can we talk?" The spirit possessing her offered me a triumphant grin.

With barely a word to me, they went off to his basement lair where I hoped the reunion didn't get loud or bloody. What should a mother do when her son insisted on being involved with a possible possessed body?

If I said anything, they'd put me back in the hospital.

Attempting normalcy, I threw on the radio and banged around the kitchen, pretending to bake. I failed. My mind was too muddled. My heart too sad.

So when my cat showed up, leaned his chin on

the island, and said, "Go see Orville," I didn't question, just put on my coat and off I went.

My former boss lived on the opposite side of town, in a log home of all things. The red roof ran in lines of steel, and the massive chimney jutted, a cemented mash of big, roundish river stones. The massive driveway in front of his place was comprised of pure gravel. I parked by a fancy car that wasn't Orville's. He had company. Maybe this new girlfriend I'd heard about.

I hadn't even made it up the steps before Orville stood in the doorway, glaring. At least, I think it was Orville. As with other people since I'd woken, he looked a little different. The demon possessing him had more height and husk, with handsome features and pointed ears. If he turned around, would I see a tail?

I should have been terrified. Run away. Instead I was relieved. A possessed Orville made sense. It explained his behavior. *It's not me that's changed, it's you.*

Now if only someone could explain why I was seeing monster auras inside regular people.

Orville, who usually had a gruff bark at best, managed a more melodious version. "What are you doing here?"

"Hi to you, too." Then because my foot fit in my mouth so well, "Why are you avoiding me?"

"Go home."

"What is wrong with you? I thought we were friends." My lip trembled. Dammit, I'd promised myself I'd be strong.

"You can't be here. Not now."

"Why not? Your girlfriend over?" I glanced at the car. "I'd love to meet her."

Apparently, Orville didn't feel the same. "Well, she doesn't want to see you. You have to go." He started down the steps, and I had to wonder at his intent. Hulking, menacing, like a bull about to charge.

I stayed out of reach, backing up a large pace for each one of his. Apparently, I had a death wish because I waved words that might as well have been a red cape. "What are you hiding?"

"Nothing. You're obviously still sick. You should go home. Rest." His reluctance must be related to the reason why Grisou sent me here.

A motion at the door showed a smaller feline sitting in its frame. Friend of my kitty's? Made me wonder how they talked.

"If nothing is wrong, then why are you acting like you're going to wring my neck?" I asked, trying not to glance at his big mitts. He might have fingers long enough to do it one-handed.

My question had him halting in his tracks. He growled, "I wish you wouldn't make this hard."

"Me? You're the one acting weird." Should I mention the fact I could see past his magical disguise? Was he an elf? He lacked that ethereal quality the on-screen elves had in *Lord of the Rings*, but at the same time, Orville wasn't Orville. Or was he? Maybe he'd been like this all along and I'd been too blind to see.

"I'm just trying to protect you."

"I'd love for you to explain what you're protecting me from."

There was a visible struggle on his face. "I can't."

"Why not?" My frustration grew, and my fists clenched. I swear, if one more person gave me the run-around, I might just go ballistic and kill them.

"It's just better that way. It won't be much longer," Orville said, his expression sad.

"Would you like to play some ominous music in there?" was my sarcastic retort. "Like seriously. What is up with everyone? My own kid was talking to Jace as if I was going to die. Yet here I am. In one piece. Not dead and not planning to die." My frustration boiled over, and a sharp wind blew out of nowhere, icing my anger.

Orville visibly rocked but stood firm. "It's time you left."

"No."

Before Orville could reply, I heard the one voice I would have never expected.

Kane's mother saying, "Let her in. It's cold outside."

27

I COULDN'T HELP BUT CAST GLANCES AT KANE'S mom, perched on the couch across from me, Orville by her side, holding her hand. She looked younger than I recalled. She had to be in her sixties at the youngest, more likely her seventies. But since the last time I'd seen her, her skin appeared smoother, her ears more pointed, and her demeanor definitely softer. She leaned into the stocky Orville, who wore comfortable slacks and a dark sweater. He had a hand on Kane's mom, offering comfort. Such a nice guy.

I couldn't help but hear Queen singing in my head, "Another One Bites the Dust." One by one, the people I'd counted on left me. The only thing I could rely on? Bacon, but that salty goodness could only keep a girl happy for so long.

When the silence stretched, it was as if I had awkward gremlins inside. I swear they made me blurt out, "I'm sorry about Kane." Way to be sensitive. Remind her about her dead son. I didn't even want to imagine the agony she was in. As it was, saying those words had my lips wobbling and my eyes watering.

"I highly doubt you're sorry." She sniffed. "Especially since everything that's happened to him is your fault."

"You can't entirely blame her, *Veronica*." The word held a hint of warning.

Veronica sniffed. "I will blame her because he wasn't supposed to be with her that night."

"A moose stepped onto the road. It was an accident." I couldn't shut up.

"I highly doubt that. Admit it, you killed him."

"Whoa, lady. That's quite the accusation. Why would I kill Kane? Hell, why would I kill anyone?" If my ex and all his vitriol couldn't get me to snap, why would I go off on Kane?

"Everyone knows he must have forced you into that car. You were supposed to be with Leviathan at midnight."

"Who is Leviathan? Are you talking about Darryl? I dumped him for being an asshole." No point in hiding it. "Kane was taking me home."

"You went willingly?" She sounded baffled.

I'd been willing both times, but I didn't think it prudent to mention that. "Kane was my rescuer."

"So why did you try to escape him?"

"I didn't. There really was a moose."

"Doesn't matter now. Because of you, he won't get to see the dawning of the next era."

"The dawning of what?"

As if suddenly realizing she'd said too much, Veronica offered me a cool smile. "I think I'm done talking to my son's murderer."

The words jabbed me. Poked me. I dug my nails into my palms, and I could have sworn the temperature in the room dropped.

"Don't you ply your witch tricks in here."

"What do you mean?" I asked on a frosted breath.

"Do something," Veronica hissed.

Orville slashed the air with his hand, and I saw the mark he created for a moment as it flashed to existence then faded. I could feel it working, fighting back against the chill.

The room returned to its previous warmth.

"How did you do that?"

"You're not the only one with magic. And I wouldn't recommend trying to use it against me." Orville stated flatly.

I shivered. "I didn't come here to cause trouble."

"And yet here you are. Were you hoping for a piece of my son's funeral cake?" Veronica spat.

I would have killed for some cake, extra icing, but I suspected Veronica would add poison if she offered it. "I should go."

"Yes, I think you should. Go home and hide. Or do as your grandmother did and try to fight us. We all know how that ended for her," Veronica snapped.

Did she just imply...? Surely, she hadn't.

With a pop, the frigid cold burst in and, on a breath that dropped icy daggers with each vowel, I said, "Did you kill my grandma?"

"Not us," Veronica hissed. "But we would have. She lied. She said she was the last, but then it turned out there was you. Can you believe she hid you? Hid you for a while even after her death. We only realized the lie when someone noticed the cottage hadn't fallen into disrepair."

"What's the cottage have to do with anything?"

"Your family is what keeps it alive."

I shook my head. "No, the sigils do."

She snorted. "Those are just marks if you don't pour magic into them."

I almost asked, whose magic, only to know the answer in that same instant. My magic.

"Once we realized someone in your family still lived, we started searching for you and ran into difficulty tracking you down. Your grandmother was quite the sorceress."

"But you did find me." I remembered the letters reminding me of the cottage. "Your family company tried to have me sell the cottage."

"We hoped to remind you of its existence and convince you to return. We knew our efforts paid off when the watcher saw the house waken."

"It knew I was coming," I muttered aloud.

"And we knew we had a chance."

"A chance to what?"

Veronica's chin lifted. "To take back that which was stolen from us. To once more touch the source of our magic."

"You can't do magic?"

Her lips turned down. "Only the original eleven can. But soon that which was taken will be returned."

It sounded like something out of a fantasy novel. The thing that didn't fit? Usually crazy quests happened to moody teenagers, not middle-aged women.

"Why are you telling me this?" Why now when

I'd been asking for answers pretty much since my arrival?

"Why not?" She shrugged.

I tried to make sense of it. "How do I fit in this? Is this about the fact I wouldn't sell you my cottage?" Did they need to own all the property around the lake to conduct a weird ritual?

"Don't bother explaining," Orville interjected. "She's clueless. I told you, Irma didn't prepare her at all." Irma being my grandma.

"How could she not have taught her? Even after her death, her magic kept so much hidden from us. Why go through that trouble and not prepare her heir?" Veronica eyed me as if she could see the answer in my face.

The epiphany emerged when I whispered, "She didn't teach me to be a witch because of my mom." Maybe Grandma feared I'd turn out to be crazy too.

The good news, I never tried to kill my kids. Doing better than her already at the mom thing.

"My grandma wanted me to have as normal of a life as possible. It's why she sent me off to college." I remembered the extra-long hug. The promise to visit often.

I hadn't meant to break it.

"In the end, even her magic couldn't fight fate.

You returned, and now our work will bear fruit." Veronica couldn't have sounded more like a villain if she tried.

"What kind of fruit? What exactly are you all waiting for? And who is this *we*? Is the whole town involved?" Veronica and Orville reminded me of the Rapture people. Anytime, anyplace, they were ready to go.

Veronica stared at me as if astonished. "Your ignorance is astounding. Do you know any of your history at all?"

I remembered the stories my grandma told me of some heroes. "Are you a *Maed'doulain'a*?" The strange word swirled sinuously off my tongue, a name for ancient heroes who battled an evil power. But in the end, the Maed'doulain'a conquered and hid the power so that the bad guys could never use it again.

"A Maed'doulain'a ?" Her laughter rang like a trill of songbirds. "Never."

I said the word I'd heard most bandied around. "Orcs."

At her sour expression, Orville stirred. "You've just insulted my people saying it like that. Our true name is *Orgh'kks.*"

I blinked. Sounded the same to me. "And what makes orkus"—"I deliberately skewed it—"different from so-called humans?" Other than the fact Orville definitely had a ghostly silhouette with pointy ears that poked from his hair. Veronica appeared one hundred percent human bitch. But inside? Definitely part troll.

"The Orgh'kks are a people who came here accidentally from another dimension and were stranded," Orville stated. Apparently, he was finally willing to talk.

My eyes widened. "Aliens."

Veronica took offense. "We are descended from superior beings."

"Says you. How diluted is that bloodline? Or is this a case of sibling intermarriage?"

Her jaw dropped, and she was indignant. "We've done an excellent job preserving our lines without familial ties. We might be small in number, but we are highly placed around the world."

"If you're so important, then why all this interest in a small town? You can't tell me the lake mud is that special." I'd been making pottery with it for weeks and couldn't say I'd noticed any of the so-called health benefits.

"That mud contains something very precious. Which, when the time is right, will return us to our former grandeur."

Was it me, or did Orville roll his eyes? "Does this have anything to do with Maddy?"

Veronica's nose wrinkled. "The guardian? I thought that thing was dead."

The reminder hit me in the gut. "She was guarding the mud? Why?"

Rather than reply, Veronica went off on another tangent. "Did you know, the moment you arrived at the cottage, there was a scramble to find bodies suitable for hosts so the Eleven could get close to you?" Veronica declared.

That went deeply crooked. "Hold on, a second. When you says hosts, are you talking about possessing people?"

"The correct term is owning," Orville said.

I glanced at him. "That sounds even worse."

Veronica's smile deepened. "Actually, it's a great honor. Imagine my pride when my son was chosen as one of the vessels. Elevated above all others, honoring our family until you killed him," she spat.

Orville put his hand on hers. "He didn't die in vain. I promise, the next honor will be coming to you." They gave each other a sappy gaze that almost made me gag.

Was everyone in love? Way to rub it in.

"What do you mean by vessel?" I asked before they started making out.

"A vessel is a willing body given over to one of the ruling eleven," she explained.

It didn't make it clearer. "Are you saying Kane has the soul of some dead guy inside him?"

"A simplistic summary at best."

"But true. Kane does have some kind of ghost inside him." Or was it more like a demon? After all they usually possessed people. Someone fetch a priest and some holy water.

"Kane was blessed by one of eleven."

I didn't like her use of the past tense. "Eleven what? Demons from another dimension?"

"The Eleven are what's left of the originals who were stranded here, who seeded the Orgh'kks line by mixing our blood with those already living in this dimension. They are the spirits of our rulers. Passed down amongst our kind so that their knowledge is not lost."

It was as if a light bulb went off, and I suddenly understood. It was in a story my grandma told me, except it was seventeen demons, not eleven, who broke out of hell and caused chaos on Earth. Fornicating and seeding the world with minions. It was up to the heroes to wipe them out because only when all the minions died would the demons die too.

Seventeen minus eleven meant six down, too

many to go and one of them in the room with me. Orville was definitely wearing a demon. Veronica wasn't, however there was no doubting the fact she hoped she'd be chosen as a vessel. Meaning there were at least ten more out there, wearing bodies, *owning* people who didn't deserve to lose their identity. We were going to need tankers of holy water.

"Why did your eleven demon ghosts want to get close to me?" Because I'd not forgotten what Veronica said.

"Your ignorance is stunning. And I tire of explaining. Begone." Veronica waved, but I was just getting started.

"You can't stop talking now." Not when I was finally getting answers. "What is the end game here? Why are the Orgh'kks invading Cambden? Is the whole town possessed?"

"Those not descended of the Orgh'kks were encouraged to leave. Those that wouldn't depart, or could be used, became hosts." Veronica smiled at Orville and a shiver went through me as I realized these eleven demon spirits could jump into anyone.

"All the new people moving into town, they're Orgh'kks?" I struggled with the pronunciation. Veronica nodded. "Why here?"

"They have come to see the return of our power." Orville stepped in.

"How did you lose it in the first place?" I tapped my chin, only it wasn't hard to see where this conversation would lead. "Let me guess. A great, great relative of mine didn't like how the Orgh'kks used their power or magic or whatever and hid it from you. I can see how they might have come to that conclusion given you have real asshole tendencies." Yeah, it felt good to say it.

Judging by Veronica's gnashing teeth, she didn't enjoy it as much. "We will take back our magic."

"Not sure that's a good idea." Because I was fairly sure they had a good reason to act as they did. Genocide and dictatorial attitudes came to mind.

"The source is ours." When Veronica appeared as if she'd launch from the couch, Orville held her back, murmuring, "Patience. It won't be long now before she's nothing and we reign supreme."

"I would have preferred she die in the crash instead of my son." Veronica proved blunt, and it worried me.

In the movies, there was one thing I knew. When the bad guys stopped hiding, it was because they thought they'd won. Veronica and Orville no longer cared what I knew, meaning either there was no escape or it was happening too soon for me to do anything about it.

Leaving me with two choices: run now, as far as

I could to try and escape, or stop whatever it was from happening. Running hadn't worked thus far, so I chose to get answers.

I snapped my fingers. "Returning to the body snatchers, you said one of them took over Kane. Which is horrible, by the way. He's your son."

Veronica's chin lifted. "He did it willingly. It is considered an honor among the Orgh'kks."

"How much of Kane was left behind?" Or was the man I'd met all demon?

"All of him, but with improvement."

So the man I'd flirted with was the demon and man. "What happens if the body dies?"

"The body dies."

"And the parasite leeching on to it?" Because if it was passed down, then it would have jumped to a new host.

"Would have jumped to a new host that hasn't made himself known yet. And it could be he's not even a he anymore. The eleven choose the shape that suits them best." Veronica sounded nonchalant about it.

"If they can choose, then why Orville and not you? Rich woman with tons of power and yet he's the one with a demon inside." I pointed out.

That brought a slow smile to Orville's lips.

"This new host was a step down from my previous one."

"Who were you before you took over Orville?" I asked.

"A man with a position in government, high enough to shift laws."

"And you dumped it to become a short order cook?" I was confused.

"He suited my needs, although, I've had to shift my vessel's mindset quite a bit. He wasn't happy to share the body."

"Is Orville still inside?"

"He is now a part of me, sharing all his knowledge and abilities. And when I move vessels, he'll move with me."

"Meaning whoever got Kane's demon spirit, will also have Kane." This all seemed wild, and yet I knew it to be true. Which again made me think of the movies. Was everything in life comparable to a show? "Why are you telling me all this?"

"Because it soon won't matter." Veronica gestured. "You're not your grandmother. You don't know how to stop us. And if you tried, we'd remove you and use the next heir. After all we made sure you had two."

Those were heart attack words, but I'm glad to say I remained alive but not well. Not well at all.

"Pretty sure you had nothing to do with my babies." I remembered pushing them out all too well.

Veronica's expression turned sly. "Did you know Martin was sterile?"

The query out of the blue threw me. "No, he wasn't." Geoff was proof, even if I wasn't sure about Winnie anymore.

"Neither of your children was fathered by him. Best we can tell he was sterilized by magic. Didn't your grandmother's recipe book have a spell for that?"

I wanted to say impossible. She'd never do that.

Only I was beginning to see there were lots of things I didn't know.

Veronica clapped her hands and laughed. "Oh my. Yet more surprises. Imagine ours when we discovered one of the eleven accidentally found you and ensured you had heirs."

"Who?" I could barely say it.

"Berith. He made sure you got impregnated, twice. He used two different Orgh'kks to do it and then hid your existence from us for the longest time. Kept an eye on you via a spell he placed on your husband."

It made me think of some of Martin's journal entries about feeling watched. They made a lot more sense now. "He's the reason Martin went crazy."

"The seed of his insanity already lingered inside."

"But this Berith triggered it. You pushed him off the edge and made him hate me. Our kids." I reeled at the strange fount of information. "You people have been manipulating me almost my entire life."

"Haven't you grasped the truth yet? We'll do anything to unlock our magic and rule the world."

28

Nothing like having your whole worldview blown apart, making you question everything.

Neither kid belonged to Martin. I'd stayed in a loveless marriage for the wrong reasons.

I left Orville and his cackling lover, feeling worse than ever. I had gone for moral support from a friend and discovered more enemies, more questions, and more danger.

I should leave town. Right now. Just keep on driving away from here and never look back. Only, while I'd made so many damned mistakes, there were two things I didn't regret. My kids.

I focused on them. I couldn't let them down. I noticed the headlights behind me followed me onto the road that ended in a cul-de-sac. Could be the driver was visiting Jace or lost.

Would a lost car have been following me since I left Orville's place? I gripped the steering wheel as they got closer. My windows frosted. I sped up. I wasn't far from home.

Almost there.

I pulled into the driveway, and the other car shot past. My instant relief had me slouching as I parked.

I'd made it home. Winnie was there with Geoff, the two of them in animated argument until I walked in.

My daughter appeared wan, my son determined. They both shut up at the sight of me.

"Glad you're both here. Pack your stuff. We're leaving," I announced.

"Mom, where have you been?" Winnie exclaimed. "We were worried sick about you."

"I'm a grown woman. Pretty sure there's no need to panic if I slip out for a few hours."

"You should be resting," my son insisted. Was it me, or did he appear a tad pale? They both were visibly nervous.

"What's up with you guys? Cat got your tongue?"

"I wish," Grisou grumbled, sauntering into view. "It's delicious when fresh."

Disturbing but not as much as the fact they obviously didn't hear my cat.

"It's nothing, Mom."

"All good," Geoff said, trying to be cooler.

"How are you, is the real question," Winnie said, leading me to a seat.

"Fine." I stared at them and tried to find a lie in their appearance. Surely, I'd have known Martin wasn't their father. Didn't they share a nose? Eyes?

I noticed the slight up tilt of their ears, not enough to make a big issue. The more I looked, the more I realized they barely had any of me in them. Two strangers in bodies I'd helped create.

They sat me down and fussed over me. Still much too nervous.

"What do you say we order in tonight? Meat on a stick with grilled vegetables." Winnie sounded way too enthusiastic.

"Delicious." My son rubbed his tummy for emphasis.

"Would you both just stop and tell me what's wrong?" I wanted to slap away their well-meaning hands.

"We were worried about you. You left and didn't tell us where you were going." Geoff placated me.

"Sorry. Next time I'll leave a note. But enough of me, we need to pack."

"Why?" my son asked.

"Because there's something wrong with this town."

"You're being silly," Winnie replied with a high-pitched laugh.

"Am I? Ever since arriving, it's been bad luck after worst luck. I'm tired of it. Tired of these games being played by the locals. Tired of the history weighing down our name. We need a fresh start."

"It's too late for that."

"No, it's not." This time I wouldn't stay in a toxic environment. I'd not suffered to make the same mistakes again. "Pack your shit. We leave in twenty minutes."

"We can't leave."

"Why not?" I yelled. "There's something wrong in this place. Wrong with our family. And if we stay…" I didn't say it, but I heard it in my head. Felt it in my bones. I would die.

My son and daughter exchanged a glance before Winnie hesitantly said, "If you want to leave, then fine. But not tonight. There's this thing we need to attend."

"Not going," I declared without hearing any

details. I was emotionally wrung out. Stick me with a fork done.

"You kind of have to."

"No, I don't." I didn't have to do shit.

"You can't refuse, Mom. It's important," Winnie insisted.

And I was doing my best to avoid it. But my children? "You know, don't you?" My kids at least had the decency to not look at me as I went on softly, "I die tonight, don't I?" I'd figured it out on the way home when the radio channel boasted about some kind of super moon. A good night for magic I'd bet.

"It's not what I want, what either of us want," my daughter exclaimed, confirming it.

I jumped to my feet. "You know someone wants to kill me and you're okay with it?" Shouldn't loving children be hustling my ass out of the door?

"No, I'm not okay with it. Especially since the new you is so great and stuff." Winnie snotted, finally looking like her mother.

"We don't have a choice, apparently," Geoff muttered. "It's you or us."

"And you chose me." A better mother wouldn't have sounded so sarcastic.

"No," Winnie cried out. "It's not like that. The thing is, if you won't participate in the ceremony, then they'll still kill you and either Geoff or I will take your place."

What kind of sick bastards would threaten my kids?

The kind who thought my family betrayed them.

Technically true. The witches in my line smacked down the Orgh'kks, rendered them powerless, then hid the secret to getting that magic back. They guarded it not only with spells of concealment, but a lake monster, and a witch guardian.

It occurred to me that my grandmother had tried to do something about it. Sent me away in the hopes of giving me a life. And failed.

The curse, that had gone on for much too long, drew me back. It ended now.

But only after I had a bath.

If I was going to my doom, then I'd damned well be wearing clean underwear and my second nicest dress. They could use the first one to bury me in after I'd told them where to go and fought my damnedest.

29

Only once I got to my room did I contemplate escape. I had a window. I could climb down, hop in my car, and go. Fuck my kids. Apparently, it was okay to toss me to the orcs.

Ungrateful brats.

I sobbed in my bath. Let myself have a good pity cry. Then I got calm. Not the calm of a pond on a windless morning, but that electrical moment of stillness before a storm crashed.

I was so centered and calm that the ice rimming my water shattered as I stood. For a moment I stared at myself in a mirror.

I glowed blue. Literally. Blue. It was kind of freaking me out because I looked like Orville with his pointy-eared demon, except, with me, it was truly inside my skin.

The house had taken on a somber cast, none of the lights getting bright. I could sense its melancholy as it helped dress me, the pants warm white wool, the short-heeled boots cute and perfect fitting. The turtleneck cashmere and soft. I'd never dressed so stylishly, or in so many light colors. What if I spilled something on it? Usually my stains ended up on my boobs and food in my cleavage—a snack for later.

To complete my ensemble, Winnie appeared, bearing a massive fur cloak, done in shades of white, gray, and cream.

"It's cold outside. This will keep you warm," she said, holding it out as a peace offering.

I almost slapped it out of her hand.

She saw my expression and her lips trembled. "I'm sorry, mom."

"Sorry, you're sacrificing me to some fucked up group of people?" I didn't soften the accusation.

"They left me and Geoff without any choice."

I didn't point out they could have volunteered in my place. In truth, better me than them. I appreciated the fact she at least looked upset about it.

"What was in those pages you cut out of the book?" I asked, not that there was a spell that would help me now.

"A spell to see the truth."

"And did you find it?"

She bit her lip. "I did, and wished I hadn't, which is why I cut those pages out and burned them."

She didn't elaborate on what she saw, and I was distracted by the watch on her wrist chiming.

Time was up.

"You need to get ready." Winnie bit her lower lip.

"Where is it happening?"

"The lake."

Big surprise. A part of me had always known I'd end up there. After all, wasn't this where my mother tried to kill me? It was why my father wanted to take me away. Why my grandma hid me so I wouldn't have to face my doom too soon. Once my grandma died, the magic concealing the source failed, the lake monster protecting it died, and the Orgh'kks ended up finding it. Now, they would sacrifice me to get it back.

But at least I'd look fashionable.

I ran my fingers over it. "It's soft. Absorbent." The blood would soak into it like a sponge.

"Mom, I—"

I interrupted her. "Don't apologize. I don't blame you. If the roles were reversed, I'd do the same. It's for the best." I placated her like I'd placated my miserable husband for a good chunk of my life.

She never suspected. I appeared docile on the outside. Cooperative, if politely refusing offers of aid in getting ready. As if I wanted help readying myself for my own funeral. I was pretty sure a turkey would say no thanks if a person asked it to give a wing/hand with the plucking.

I sent everyone away because it gave me time to think. Surely there was a way out of this madness.

A spell. I dug out everything I had. The oddly inert ring my grandma left me. It felt like cheap metal on my finger.

With an eyeliner I dug out, I wrote sigils on my body that might protect me. It couldn't hurt. I slipped chalk into my bra, just in case. Sent up a small prayer to the two people I knew loved me most. "Grandma, Dad, if you're listening…" What could I say? "I love you." Might see you soon. Because how could I fight this alone?

Even a superhero would be hard-pressed given everyone around worked against me.

As I went down the stairs it was to see the main floor lined with people in cloaks, the hoods drawn up, hiding their features in shadow. Except for Geoff and Winnie. They stood side by side, also in black with voluminous cloaks, looking anxious. No mistaking the big shape standing possessively by my daughter. Jace. A man who'd convinced her it was in her best interest to sacrifice me. Was he that good in bed?

Outside, more robed figures awaited, forming a path down to the lake. The cold proved brisk, but I welcomed the sharp bite. As long as I felt it, I lived.

We marched to our destination with Geoff on one side of me, Winnie the other. A few paces behind, Jace and Helena.

Partners in crime? They felt more like hostage takers than lovers. Had my children yet realized they'd had their hearts fooled?

And for what?

I still had to wonder what they thought killing me would do. Whatever they'd lost, I had no idea how to find it.

At the edge of the lake sat a sledge made of a marble-like material that sucked in the light of the rising moon. I didn't want to get in. Getting in meant accepting my fate. Getting in meant I'd die so my kids would live. Was there really any other choice?

I couldn't run. But maybe I could—

Before I'd managed to hit the ground, reaching to trace, my arms were grabbed. Hard. Painful enough I gasped more in shock at who held me.

"Geoff." He didn't look at me as he marched me to the sledge.

No apology as he thrust me in. I huddled on the seat. Stunned. Sad.

Despite there being no animals tethered to it, the sledge slid amidst an eerie silence broken only by the hiss of the blades over ice as magic dragged me to my doom.

Toward the hole. The very same spot my mother tried to drown me in.

It wasn't glowing. Not anymore. The light came from the people who'd gathered. It lit them from within, and I felt an answering tug. As if I knew that light.

Wanted it.

As I passed the watching crowd, I saw the bottles of mud, packaged in the mill, lying on the ice. The contents smeared on skin—face, hands, clothes—glowing for some reason.

I faced forward again as the sledge managed a graceful turn and stop. There were nine people standing, waiting. Some I knew like Orville and Trish—fucking Trish was possessed? Since when? Or had she been like this since my return and I'd not noticed?

Did Jojo know?

The question had me glancing to the watching

crowd and spotting Marjorie in the front ranks, her expression beatific. Not a care in the world. Obviously in cahoots with the bad guys.

Back to the nine, it also included Jace and Helena—who I'd bet was the one whispering in Martin's ear, getting him to snap. And now, she'd moved on to my son.

There were faces I didn't know, nor would I find out because Darryl, the one I wanted to see least, stood by the sledge and offered a hand.

I could see the demon clearly atop his body. A much bigger and more handsome version. Pointed ears and horns. He grinned. I didn't let him see my shudder and avoided his help as I stepped out.

My super-sized cat sat among the nine, not demon possessed but also not my friend as I'd thought. Part of the plot against me. The final dagger in my heart.

It left no one to care how scared I was. No one to fight for me.

I could do this. Be brave. I wanted to be, but I dared the strongest people to face certain death without some kind of regret. I bowed my head as tears welled.

"That's no good. She's like a fucking martyr," muttered Helena. She stood beside Orville, her red hair peeking from the hood.

"She won't be feeling sorry for herself for long. Bring him out," snapped Darryl.

The crowd shifted, and someone was carried over, the hood over their head covering their face, their limbs bound in chains.

My heart stopped.

I knew even before they dropped him by my feet. I fell to my knees. "Kane?"

The person jerked and yanked their wrists hard enough to snap the chains. The hood came off, and a bruised Kane stared at me.

Number eleven.

"Ah fuck, sweetheart." Such reassuring words to match his bleak expression.

Boom.

Like a thunderclap, the noise drew attention so that in the quiet that followed I clearly heard Darryl say, "Dearly beloved, and most hated enemies, we are gathered here today to finally put an end to our curse. To regain our magic. Today, the Orgh'kks rise again."

Combine that speech with the dagger in Darryl's hand? Today Naomi dies.

30

KNOWING THE DEMON-POSSESSED WANTED ME DEAD, I expected something gruesome. A horrible, horrible death.

Panic hit me.

"Kane." For a teeny, tiny second when he held me close, I thought things might turn out all right.

It didn't last. Kane turned from me and held out his hand.

Darryl slapped the dagger into it. "You know what to do."

Kane was going to kill me? Every single person watching us was hoping for a soap opera ending.

"Kane?"

He wouldn't meet my gaze.

"Coward." I couldn't help but say it. To feel

angry. I held my ground as he moved to stand in front of me. Bruised. Obviously in pain. Some of the injuries fresh.

He stared at me then the dagger, his hand flexing on the hilt.

I had to ask. "Why sleep with me if the plan was always to kill me?"

"Because emotion unlocks deeper magic."

And what deeper than the betrayal of a lover. A lover who hesitated to murder me.

"Who tortured you?" I asked on impulse because the car crash had happened a month ago. The bruise on his jaw wasn't that old.

"Do you really have to ask? This moment has been centuries in the making." He lifted his gaze to the sky, to the planets almost in perfect alignment. "I showed weakness and was reminded of my duty."

"Weakness how?

"Because I wanted to find another way. A way that didn't kill you." He ignored the hiss from those eavesdropping.

"You wanted me alive. Why?" Why was I torturing myself asking these questions? It didn't matter now.

"Because I fell in love with you," he said softly.

My knees wobbled.

Full emotional impact achieved.

"Oh. Kane." I whispered his name just as the star and planets shifted into their rarely seen place. The moon beamed, bathing me with cold. So cold, and yet when I cupped his cheek, heat filled me. "You have a weird way of showing your love."

"It wasn't supposed to be me. But then that night…I couldn't resist you." His expression turned bleak.

I didn't need to ask whose spot Kane had taken. Darryl thought he'd be the one to kill me. Now it had to be Kane. Given the choice, I'd rather have my lover do it. Let him bear the guilt.

Seriously. What was wrong with the people who loved me? Did no one want to save me?

Fine.

I'd save myself.

I screamed to the sky, an incoherent rambling that fed the eagerness of the crowd.

"Calm down." Trish, my former best friend, now wearing a demon spirit with not only pointed ears but fanged teeth, thought she could dispense advice. "Do you want the legends to remember you died a screaming coward?"

"Open the gate."

"Yeah. Open it."

The dual yells drew my attention to a sigil on the ground. How had I not noticed it before? It was huge and intricate. A whorl that circled the hole in the ice. A complicated spell waiting to be activated. Waiting for my death.

"Can I have one last request?"

"Hurry it up, the moon is almost in position," Darryl snapped.

"What?" Kane asked, knowing I spoke to him.

"Kiss me hard so I don't feel the blade going in."

He recoiled from my words. He didn't fake the pain in his eyes. Then he grabbed me close, pressing his mouth to mine.

But I'd lied. I didn't want a kiss. I whispered, "I wish you'd loved me enough."

His murmured reply, "Who says I don't? I won't kill you." He threw himself away from me. "Do you hear me? She doesn't have to die for this to work."

"We need a conduit and we need blood," his mother snapped, bossy for someone without a demon of her own. I guess having a son who was possessed gave her some power.

"Then use me." Before I could grasp his intent, Kane cut himself.

"What are you doing?" I gasped.

He hit the ground on his knees and held out his bleeding arm over the sigil. His gaze met mine. "Saving you."

"They'll still kill me." I could hear the discontent. A mob who would tear me limb from limb.

"Not if you give them what they want. Funnel the spell through me."

"What spell? I don't know any." I huffed in a panic. "I thought the ritual needed my blood to work."

"The spell needs your Earth based magic, but any blood can start the process."

"I don't know what to do," I wailed.

"Just go with your instinct. Use me. Think of me as the battery."

I couldn't. I wouldn't. The people around us began to boo, their anger palpable.

Something had to be done. A glance to my side showed Darryl staring at the moon. We'd not reached the full peak of it.

I dove on Kane and slapped a hand over the gash in his wrist. As if I'd closed a connection, the sigil ignited, if weakly.

Fizzled. And wobbled.

About to extinguish.

Kane pushed me away. "There's still time.

287

Quick before the spell collapses. We don't have much time. The planets are aligning."

"No." I shook my head.

He mouthed, *Love you, sweetheart.*

Before I could blink, a sword burst through his chest.

31

DARRYL STOOD BEHIND HIM, SMIRKING. Triumphant. As Kane slumped, bleeding out over the pattern, Darryl aimed a sword at me.

"Cry, witch. Cry for your lover. It will make the magic more powerful."

"What is wrong with you?" I exclaimed. "Did your mother not hug you as a child?" I huffed, icy rage and despair filling me.

"What will you do, witch? Nothing. Because I will kill you and drain you." A cry drew my attention to my daughter being held in a headlock by her boyfriend.

She clawed at his arm, squealing, "Let me go."

Jace sound almost apologetic as he said to Winnie, "If I do, you'll die with her."

"I'm okay with that," Darryl drawled.

A bitchy mom would have said, something smart ass like, *Hey kids, guess you wished we'd left when I said we should.*

But I only had a moment to live. A second to do something.

Anything.

My emotions roiled, a tempest in a Naomi-pot, about to burst free in a hiss of angry steam. The angrier I got, the more the temperature dropped, and I remembered what the spell had shown me when I asked who controlled The Chill.

Me.

A magic that didn't require a sigil to wield. It came because my chaotic emotions called it. It was mine, and I wanted to use it.

Let's start a fight.

By accepting it, I invited it into me. The thing the magic had been trying to do all along. The magic my grandma left me. It finally came home. Filled me with strength.

The temperature plummeted, and people noticed.

Every breath fogged. My anger, my pain, my everything turned cold. The Chill was me, my emotions taking shape. Whisked out of me to leave me frozen inside.

"You shouldn't have killed Kane." The words were an icy mist.

"Even now you would forgive him?" Darryl sneered. "Weak. Like the rest of your family."

"More like tempered steel, mother fucker," I muttered, watching as Darryl's dagger began its arc as if in slow motion.

"Today is not a good day to die. For me. In case that wasn't clear…" I faded off on my ruined heroic speech and dropped to my knees to put my hand on the mark carved into the ice. They'd run it deep, making it into a channel that filled with Kane's blood. It throbbed, wanting to release the spell, but it needed one more ingredient.

Me.

Only they'd not counted on me being alive when I was added.

I blew ice, and the fire in the sigil lines frosted.

"What are you doing?" Darryl exclaimed, lifting his dagger for try number two.

"You don't mind if I make some modifications, do you?"

Darryl didn't like that one bit. His arm went to slash, only to find out Kane wasn't quite dead. He threw himself at Darryl, and the pair of them hit the ground and rolled, grunting. The blood ignited even more of the circle.

The matrix ignited all the way around the hole. The atmosphere electrified.

Darryl stood and kicked Kane's limp body. He smirked, and everything in me froze. The very air hung in chilly silence.

"Your turn to bleed," he said, waggling his knife.

"No." One of the most assertive things I ever said, because in that moment I understood I had a few choices.

I could do nothing. Simply let Darryl slice my throat and use me to open some mystical door to another dimension.

Die without a fight?

I'd rather smite these assholes using my magic. I didn't figure I needed to kill them all, just their demon-possessed leaders. That was probably the most sensible course since the portal would remain closed.

On the other hand, the peeved minions would probably kill me. Possibly my kids, too. And for what?

To prevent the Orgh'kks from getting their hands on some magic? Why should I care?

It was as if my grandmother suddenly stood beside me and every single story she'd ever told me merged into one. I finally understood and said slowly, "The Maed'doulain'a were the ones who took away your magic. Locked it away." They used their innate Earth magic to protect against the invaders.

"Meddling bastards," was the sneered reply.

"Only because you harmed my world." I could suddenly see it, see how the original seventeen fled a dying world by coming into mine, bringing their magic and violence.

"They had no right to hide the source of our power."

A secret my family guarded for centuries until I failed.

And now, because of my inability to see before now, I'd die.

Unless...

"What if I cooperated?" I said, eyeing the illuminated sigil. "You don't have to kill me to open a gateway to that other world."

"But killing you is the fun part. I can't wait to taste your blood."

I'd had just about enough of psycho Darryl. My words like icy daggers, I said, "You want magic. I'll give you magic." Unlike the eleven, I didn't need blood or the shape on the ground.

I spoke in words I didn't understand but that thundered.

The world disappeared in a blaze of white light. I sucked in a breath and closed my eyes. Behind the lids I could see the outline of two doors. One a tiny ragged tear barely patched together. I was more interested in the full portal covered in sigils. Warnings. So many cautions that I ignored.

It called to me. Begged me to open it. I threw cold, arctic power at it, trying to slice open that spot between the worlds. The magic hit the door and dispersed against it with a discordant squeal that made the world scream. I strained the very bounds of strength trying to open the door, but it wouldn't budge.

I heard a voice shouting, *"She's trying to open the full gate."*

"No, she can't."

"Don't let her."

"We can only contain a small piece."

Small piece of what? I wondered.

"She'll destroy us all."

Would I? Why should I care when they were all willing to sacrifice me?

I eyed the portal and realized there was a lock in the center of it.

Guess who was the key?

THE MILLISECOND I STUFFED MY SPIRIT INTO THAT lock, I realized I might have erred.

For one, there was a reason they'd carved a tiny door. Something waited on the other side, and when the portal opened, it blew past me in a fury.

I could only watch as the magical storm I'd unleashed shot off in different directions, seemingly random until I realized some of the glowing people got brighter.

As if a beacon, the furious spirit went after the brightest of the Orgh'kks, buffeting them, scouring the glow from their flesh and drawing yelps. It was hard to feel anything but sympathy; after all, the Orgh'kks chose to wear the mud containing the decaying remains of an angry spirit.

It was amazing how much I understood too late.

The Orgh'kks never had magic of their own. They'd stolen it by creating a small portal to another other dimension. Somehow, they trapped a piece, the equivalent of a human limb, from a being of power, a portion of it, anyhow. Used it to give them magic.

The original seventeen fled their world, and, when Earth's magic eluded them, sought a new source of power. They found it and caused trouble, enough that my ancestors slammed the door shut to their magic, cutting off the source. The part they'd stolen, became inert and was hidden in the lake by my ancestors, waiting for the day when the portal opened again and it could be reunited with the rest of itself.

What the Orgh'kks didn't count on? The being noticed the theft. And it was pissed.

The Orgh'kks had thought the mud imbued with the esoteric remains would make them powerful. That when the door opened, they'd be given the magic, the eleven promised.

Instead, it marked them for death.

Calling what entered my world a ball of energy was too simplistic. There was method to its fury. Cold calculation as it swept and gathered all its stolen pieces. For one stupid moment, the idiots on the ice cheered. They thought this was a good thing. That I'd brought their magic back.

Fools. What I'd actually done was given what was stolen back to its owner and then handed the thieves to the seething entity on a platter of ice.

The cheering stopped when the lake's cold covering cracked. A chunk of it— with people still on it— disappeared below the water.

That was when the screaming started.

33

THE CYNICAL PART OF ME WATCHED THE PANIC, unmoved. For fuck's sake. What did they think might happen, having that many people on ice only a few weeks old? Then I remembered how they all stood there watching me going to my doom, rooting for my death.

Remember the Good-bye song? I would have sung it if I didn't have more important things to worry about than drowning Orgh'kks. I was kind of busy holding open a door and trying to figure out how to let go without dying in the process.

The glow left the lake, and silence fell. Eerie silence that saw people not daring to move lest more of them plunge into the icy depths. Those that fell in the water and sank? I imagine hypothermia killed them before they drowned. But I didn't have time to worry about it.

I might have peed myself a little when *it* exploded: a thing without true shape or sound, yet all could see it, a cloud of pure magic that spoke without words.

I AM WHOLE.

"What is that?" someone muttered.

The cloud suddenly had dark pits for eyes, a dozen of them, and it narrowed in on the speaker before it boomed. *I AM GOD.*

A whiner in the crowd also felt a need to speak up. "What happened to our magic?"

A different idiot pointed an accusing finger. "That thing stole it. Give it back."

Big fog god loomed suddenly at the idiot's level. *YOU WANT. I GIVE.*

The cloud fist slammed the speaker flat like a rock had dropped from space.

The good news? He didn't feel a thing. The bad? The fog god wasn't done. *WHO. NEXT.*

No one else said a word, but me.

"Listen here, demon fog monster, I brought you into this world, and if I have to, I'll take you out of it."

YOU DARE.

The fog god tried to intimidate me. Me, a

woman who'd now faced down death numerous times and won. When would I be taken seriously?

I glared right back. "Don't you sass me."

I AM GOD.

"If you say so. I'd like proof." I pointed to Kane. "Fix him."

I DO NOT—

"I didn't ask for excuses. I asked for proof. You say you're god, then bring him back," I snapped.

The fog suddenly invaded Kane's pores in ways that were probably painful. His body jerked. Then twitched. I didn't relax until I saw the whites of his eyes and he said, "What the fuck happened?" I'd take that over him asking for brains.

I wanted to throw myself at him, but I still had a god to deal with. Not to mention, I was kind of stuck in a door.

"So, um, god, now that you've gotten all your pieces back, you should go home," I suggested.

NO.

It was like dealing with a stubborn child, or a middle-aged man.

"This isn't your world."

MINE.

The temper tantrum rattled the ice, and there was screaming as chunks splintered and people slipped under.

Why, oh why were they all standing there still? Did they not see everything had gone awfully sideways?

Kane rose to his feet and flexed before looking at me. "We need to close the door."

How cute he said we. "I'm open to suggestions that don't involve me dying."

"Close it the same way your ancestors did it."

"Any ideas how they did that?"

"Your magic."

The magic, which was currently stuffed in the lock. Was it as simple as me yanking it out?

"I'm going to close it," I felt a need to warn. After all, the last time my family shut it, we kind of cut off the fog demon's hand, although I wanted to say tentacle because it had come through a small door.

NO.

I withdrew, closing the door slowly, wedging the shape extending out from it. How much was on the other side?

"You can't stay here. You're dangerous."

MAKE DEAL.

For a second, I almost told it to fuck off. I could easily shut the door and lock it. Yeah, me and my kids would still be the only way to open it. Meaning we'd still be cursed. Or we could kill everyone on the ice and make sure there was no one left to hurt us.

I looked at the god I'd brought into the world and said, "What kind of a deal are you thinking?"

What followed was my bargain with the devil. I negotiated, even threatened a bit, I won some concessions, I gave god a few. In the end, though, I'd done one truly important thing.

I ended the curse on my family line and remained alive to enjoy it. But I wasn't sure I'd be talking to my kids unless they really upped their game this Mother's Day.

34

One conquered world later—which, for the curious, took less than seventy-two hours. God knew how to put on a show for the masses.

WANT.

"It's not ready yet." I slapped the god's smoky hand before he could touch the cooling cookies. Low carb peanut butter with Lily chocolate chips.

My god didn't smite me, and he knew better to threaten, given I was the only thing keeping the door wedged open and his magic fed. Slam it shut and it would severe the tie and he'd be separated from a part of himself until someone opened it again.

More than five hundred years, give or a take a few as it turned out. I'd finally managed to get my hands on the missing books. And what do you know, the one that wouldn't open before finally let me read it. It was the story my grandmother told me in pieces, but in a way that told me everything I needed to know, too late.

Then again, my way had turned out pretty good.

I'd saved the world, returned magic to it, kind of. God was picky about who he gifted with power. For example, most of the eleven? Didn't get any. Like Darryl. Not only did he not get magic, he lost his demon spark. New god ate it leaving him a mundane human again. As for the remaining princes? They scattered.

I saw Darryl from time to time when I went to the station to gas my car or buy lottery tickets. He hid in the back, pot belly rounder than ever, and he'd lost most of his hair. Did he remember the time from his possession? Me?

I honestly didn't care.

Thinking I was doing the right thing, I tracked down Trish with the goal of having her exorcized, only to have her freak out because apparently, she really liked her demon. Too bad. I wasn't leaving my best friend possessed.

Trish pouted after and told me to never speak to her again. That hurt, especially given all the stuff she'd done to manipulate me. Had Trish forgotten her part in trying to get me sacrificed?

Jojo told me to give her time. I would, but at the same time was looking into a spell to see if I could ease the distance between us. This time round, I wasn't giving up our friendship so easily.

Orville also lost his demon to a young senator going places. Without it, he became reclusive and while he wouldn't look me in the eye, he continued to make special dishes obviously created with me in mind. While I knew he remembered us being friends, with his demon gone, it wasn't the same, this version being a shadow of the man I'd grown to love and respect.

While I had lost my shop, I didn't lack for a job. As the world had to deal with a new normal—hustled along by thousands of headlines in the media freaking about the end of the world—I became the priestess of a new religion and main wrangler of a god prone to throwing temper tantrums. It might have taken more out of me if I'd not had Kane at my back.

I wasn't the only one with a title and a job with the new god—who decided he wanted to be called george. No caps. Kane—who kept his inner demon after making a blood vow—was the priest in charge of handling heretics and skeptics. It should be noted the punishment was unconventional, and cruel. So very cruel and involved "Baby Shark." Just gonna drop that and leave it there.

My children ended up having to grovel quite a bit before I forgave them—and insisted they dumped their respective partners. Eventually, I gave them roles in the new order that put them above everyone but me or Kane. A man who'd given his life for me.

Valentine's Day was going to cost me a fortune if I hoped to compare.

I was enjoying life to the fullest, the sex still as good as the first time, although I wasn't sure anything would beat the sex we had the first night george bestowed our magic. Which I will add, only added to the magic I already had naturally, making me uber powerful.

Me. The ass-kicking, butt-saving hero of the story. But that only sank in later. At the time, when everything happened, I was as stunned as everyone else, awash in the adrenaline and power, on a sheet of cracking ice.

I recalled how Kane, alive if in need of new clothes, grinned at me and said, "That was unexpected."

"Just a little." Funny how I suddenly felt shy.

"With george checking out his new digs, what

do you say we get out of here?"

Good plan. He held out a hand, and I clasped it. We walked to the first chasm in the ice, where he waved a hand to create hard steps that hovered atop the cold water. We used them all the way to shore.

Given I wanted my kids to have a chance to grovel for forgiveness, I copied his magic and flung a set for them to use from the ice floe they were trapped on. I thought about tossing some magical life rings to the stragglers struggling in the water.

Kane shook his head. "This is their punishment for thinking they could imprison a god." Look at him, a company man already. george would be happy.

But who was going to clean up the bodies when they washed up on my beach? And someone would have to explain what happened to Officer Murphy.

As we reached shore, I saw my cat, a normal size again, sitting away from the water, licking a wet spot.

"You!" I jabbed my finger in his direction. "You were one of them the entire time."

He glanced at me, sniffed, and stalked off.

Had I lost my ability to hear him?"

Did it really matter? Hell yeah it did. Fucker betrayed me. No more wet food for him.

Kane tugged me away from the crowd on the

beach, the whole town plus some extras. Odd how they didn't spill into the woods but remained along the shoreline.

"Your house is keeping them away," Kane said, answering my not even spoken question.

Good, because I had no intention of inviting them in for a tea or anything else. Only one person who attempted to murder me was allowed inside. And that was so I could smack Kane and give him hell for lying to me before he begged my forgiveness via the exchange of sexual pleasure.

My cozy home. From the outside it kind of resembled a large log cabin chalet—my visit to Orville having obviously impressed me—threw open its front door to welcome us.

My cat sat on the rug at the entrance and gave me the once-over and meowed. His hungry meow.

I glared. "Traitor."

"I never betrayed you."

Look at that. I could still hear Grisou. "Maybe not but you also never explained fuck all." I wasn't about to give him quarter.

"It wasn't my place."

"You would have let me die."

"And yet you didn't. Congratulations."

I glared. "What are you?"

"Hungry. Fetch me some sustenance," was his imperious reply.

I wanted to boot him out of my house, instead I grumbled, "I just got home. Chill."

"I will not chill. Feed me." He weaved around my ankles.

"You can't order me around. I'm a priestess to a god now," I said.

"And I am george's confidant. Putting me above you. Open me a can of tuna, human."

I obeyed, mostly because arguing just delayed the hands that kept touching me. Kane hadn't stopped since we'd left the lake. I wanted to be alone with him.

But of course, by the time I gave the cat some food, Geoff came slamming in. My handsome boy who appeared to be ignoring the redhead at his back. "Go away, Helena."

"Geoff, we need to talk about this."

He whirled on her. "Nothing to talk about. You only ever dated me because of my family. You never cared for me."

"Not true."

"You held a knife to my heart. Literally."

"So did he, and your mother forgives him," she exclaimed, jabbing a finger at Kane.

"Kane died for me. Would you have done the

same?" was my sweet reply. I didn't like Helena, so I was more than happy when my son turned his back to say, "Leave him alone."

Helena reached for him, and that was when mama bear, me, stepped in. I didn't need to use a symbol anymore to channel my magic. I just needed to aim it and control it. In this case, slap down Helena's hand and start bum rushing her to the door.

Her wide eyes slid past me as I waved, "Buh-bye." The door slammed shut behind her, and I glanced at my house. "Make sure she doesn't come back, would you?"

The agreement proved instant.

Geoff stared at me. Throat working. "Listen, Mom. I'm—"

"Sorry? Sure, you are. I don't blame you. I mean I haven't exactly been the model parent. I blame your dad. Your real dad."

His eyes widened. "What's that supposed to mean?"

"You and your sister apparently were conceived by one of the eleven spirits inhabiting human bodies."

Geoff got stuck on, "Martin's not my dad?"

"Nope. The name of your father was Berith." I

held up a hand. "Don't ask me anything else, because I only know his name."

"*The* Berith?" Kane exclaimed.

I glanced over. "You know him? Of course, you know him. You were all part of the original magic-stealing assholes." I glared at him.

He at least had the grace to look sheepish. "Does it help if I say I never thought I'd care for you?"

"You lied to me."

"I lied to everyone so they wouldn't know I watched over you. Wouldn't realize I'd come to care for you."

"If you care so much, why weren't you trying to get me to leave like Jace?"

"Because I knew it wouldn't work. Let me ask, each time he told you to go, what happened?"

"It made me more determined to stay."

"Exactly." A wry reply.

"And the fighting between you and Jace? Are you even brothers?" Because I'd not forgotten their animosity.

"Not related by blood but by shared history. Our rivalry began long ago."

I still didn't understand so much. "Why didn't Berith let everyone know he'd found me?"

"Because he probably hoped to control you or

the children in the end. Only his perfidy, once discovered, resulted in him losing rank."

"Okay, since you have an answer for everything explain why the attempts to kill me if you needed me alive?"

"Some of it was because your magic was locked away too tight and it was thought strong emotion would help release it. And then there were those working against the plan in place. Who wanted you out of the way that they might use your children."

"Like Helena," I surmised.

He nodded. "She wanted to be the one wielding the power when the planets aligned. Hence why she turned Martin against you."

"Because with me out of the way, she could use Geoff," I muttered.

"Had she killed you directly, it would have caused a power struggle."

As the truth spilled, more questions bubbled. But one rose above the others. "How sorry are you for lying to me?"

He drew me close. "Sweetheart, I—"

The door slammed open and in stalked my daughter. She whirled and shut it. Locked it and glared.

"Where's Jace?" I asked.

"Not here obviously."

"I should hope not since you dumped him."

"Who says I dumped him?" Winnie asked.

"Seems obvious given the whole betrayed you and tried to kill you thing."

"Kind of the pot calling the kettle something rude, don't you think?" She eyeballed Kane's hand on my hip.

"But Kane didn't go through with it."

"Neither did Jace!" she huffed.

"Then why are you mad at him?" I exclaimed, utterly confused.

"Would you believe he chose schmoozing with that big thundercloud over victory sex with me?" Which turned out to be the end of his demon, but I only found that out later.

Speaking of victory sex… I glanced at Kane. Did my frustration show?

He winked at me. Then cleared his throat. "Since you appear to be in need of a celebration, then why not assuage it with ice cream? The parlor on Main Street keeps a key under the front mat."

"Did you just tell me to break into a place?"

He rolled a shoulder. "Technically, I own it. And you are a high acolyte to george."

Winnie nodded. "It should come with free ice cream. Good thinking."

"Do you like ice cream?" he suddenly asked.

"Who doesn't?" I rolled my eyes and then, because it was the kind of thing you asked, "What flavor is your favorite?"

"Vanilla."

My nose wrinkled. "It's so plain."

"I don't need fancy things to be happy."

"Did you just call me plain?" I arched a brow.

"Like hell. You are the most complicated woman I've met. It would have never occurred to me to negotiate with george. My plan once I saw him was more along the lines of beg for my life or run screaming."

I pshawed, playing it off as I explained my logic. "What's the point of being a god without worshippers?"

"Speaking of worshipping." Kane tossed me over his shoulder. Like literally swept me off my feet and carried me upstairs to the sound of Winnie whistling, "You get some, Mom."

"What are you doing?" I squealed.

"Taking you upstairs for seduction."

If I wasn't upside down, I would have taken him right then and there. But instead, I was bounced on the bed where he tossed me.

As he approached, his hands weaved, and my clothes disappeared. Left, right. Leaving me naked and exposed. I couldn't help but cover myself. But he grabbed my hands and tugged them away.

"Never hide from me."

He then stripped and showed me a body that had also seen life. Scars that I'd one day know the story about.

But I saw strength in him too. Virility. And most of all, love. When his body covered mine, I welcomed it. I kissed him, and I didn't need him inside me to have my first mini orgasm. He felt me quiver and growled.

"Wait for me."

My legs parted, and he slid between them, hard and hot, thick and ready. He thrust into me, and I clung to him, feeling my pleasure coiling, a scalding cold that met his spinning hot.

We exploded together hard enough the house shook.

He held me as we came down off our cloud, and I traced symbols on his chest.

I had to ask, "What happens next?"

"Anything you want," was his whisper.

"Anything?" I drew him closer. "I kind of want ice cream."

EPILOGUE

INTRODUCING A WILD MAGIC TO THE WORLD, ONE very different from that already present, started a chain reaction, and no surprise, things didn't end up as expected. Yes, I had kind of brought a new god into the world, but in order to keep him strong, I had to leave the door in the lake open. I soon realized george wasn't the only thing that got out, which didn't please our god at all, especially since the last time it happened, my ancestors suddenly found themselves brimming with the power needed to slam the door shut and cut off the source.

Which answered the question of how my family became witches.

Because I could do it again, george played nice.

God killer and god maker. Kind of a lofty title, but did I get any respect from my boyfriend?

Kane snuck up behind me and grabbed my ass. He also kissed my neck, and if I wasn't worried I'd burn the taco meat, I would have turned around and made use of the kitchen island for something other than chopping vegetables.

"I love taco Tuesday," he growled into my skin. My big powerful warlock, putty in my hands because of seasoned meat.

"You only stick around because of my cooking," I teased. I no longer questioned why this man could love me, because, funny thing, he worried about my ability to love him. He claimed that since I was second only to a god that he wasn't good enough for me. Which led to oral sex until I screamed he was a god.

"You know the cooking is the only reason I stay," he agreed, giving my skin a nibble. I sighed and leaned into his embrace.

"And here I was going to say I only keep you around for the sex."

"It is very good sex," he agreed, and I laughed.

"The news today mentioned something about dragons appearing in the Andes," I said, remembering the tidbit I'd seen.

He stilled. "How did it escape without us seeing it?"

We'd been tracking the things coming out of the

317

lake, like Maddy number two. I'd already formed a bond with the baby lake monster. I couldn't wait to show Kane the tricks it could do.

I didn't mention some of the leakage was my fault. I'd told george that the world could use more fantasy instead of reality. I think the god took that to mean dragons and unicorns. What was next? A ring to bind them? A kitchen boy with a pig? A tomb raider with the best hair?

Maybe it would be me. Who said my journey was done. After all, I wasn't even close to halfway there with all the things I wanted to do. I was on my way to having the best happily ever after, so long as I didn't stop believing.

Despite the odds, I found the magic in the heart of me and changed the world.

The End

FOR MORE EVE LANGLAIS BOOKS (INCLUDING SOME WITH SEASONED HEROINES) PLEASE VISIT EVELANGLAIS.COM